Twisting Tentacles

Arian Mabe

This is a collection of short stories focusing on tentacle erotica.

This story collection includes: cisgender characters, transgender characters, humans characters, anthropomorphic characters, straight sex, gay sex, lesbian sex, tentacles, vines, oral sex, vaginal sex, anal sex, oviposition, egg and cum inflation and sex outdoors.

Cover art by Alena Bodrova.

Table of Contents

Taking a Tentacle Monster
(Female)   6

Trapped by the Tentacles
(Female)   17

Lustful Experimentation
(Female)   28

Bound Luxury
(Female)   39

Tentacle Play
(Female)   50

Their Tentacle Toy
(Female, multiple characters)   58

Tentacle Dreams
(Male)   73

His Special Plant
(Male)   84

Deep in the Cavern
(Male)   101

A Fine Feline
(Male)   118

A Dragon of the Deep
(Male and male)   129

Playing with Magic   147
(Male and female)

The Spell   164
(Transgender male)

Out in the Water   172
(Transgender female)

Taking a Tentacle Monster

Morticia gasped, standing on the precipice to the abyss, staring into the heart of which the tentacle monster lurked. Deep in the darkest depths of the ocean – yet still reachable by natural phenomenon. Or unnatural phenomenon, depending on what one considered natural or not in the world. The dragoness anthro was unnatural to some too but natural otherwise, her pale gold scales layered softly over her body as if she had skin there rather than scales: they were simply that fine. Two horns rose in a sensual arch from her narrow, fine, refined muzzle, eyes delicate and daring in a splash of pink.

She was a beauty, light on her feet, toes tipped with claws. Morticia would have done well by anyone, a mane of soft pink hair falling down the back of her neck, but she was more interested in the tentacle monster, a fall of water diving straight into the ocean from the boat where she stood, bobbing tenaciously. The pool that had formed there was as if a cliff had been cut through the water itself, dropping sharply into darkness, nothingness, the froth and foam of the ocean dropping away more than she could take.

"I'm coming…"

The dragoness exhaled softly, salt crystals forming on her scales in tiny specks of white, the moisture dampening her bare hide. Her breasts were large and full, though not as often as on complete display as they were there. Yet it was not as if there was anyone else at all out there to bear witness to her fragile nudity, no nipples present on her mammary glands, which had developed on her species of dragon for show in an anthro society, rather than for any function.

Her tail lashed. The tentacle monster did not care about that and neither did she, hair lifting from the back of her neck as the ocean breeze gusted up.

Down there, in the pit of water, the cliff edge dropping off before her eyes, as she stood there, poised perfectly, there was no going back. Morticia would only ever be able to return to the boat again if the tentacle monster let her go, though the dragoness was not all that sure anyway that she even wanted to be let go, once she was wrapped up in their devious, twisting coils.

One deep breath, salt on her lips. The stormy sky roiled above, but the clouds were merely a threat with no promise behind them. Morticia exhaled. And her body went right along with that exhalation of breath.

She didn't quite understand the moment between standing there and falling, but Morticia was aware, in some way, that she had jumped. Falling and shrieking, the whistling sea wind whipped words from her lips, though they could only ever have been words of joy and passion, her tail twisting and curling behind her even as she fell.

The air caressing her body tickled and pulled, itching at her scales, yet that deeper course of passion was what rose up within her, the burning heat of arousal that could never be simmered down by any manner of cold. That was why Morticia had to seek out the tentacle monster, the heat of arousal driven up between her thighs already. And it was not even a sense of exotic eroticism that even her tail or the largest, most dominant of partners could satisfy, even if she'd wanted to try that course again.

No…

Morticia moaned, something shifting below her, the surface of the ocean oh so far away already as she fell. He was close, yes, so very close. She'd never go back to something that was not satisfying, at least not to her.

Never again.

The monster rushed up to meet her, a twisting grind of green and blue tentacles – there was even some grey and yellow in the mass of them! She had wanted to get a better look at the monster that she was willing to give herself over to, but it was too late, a tentacle lashing out and up, winding around her tightly. It secured her midsection and then not even her fall was under her control anymore, dragging her down into the midst of its depths, the writhing tentacles squirming wetly over her, slick as if with their own lubrication.

Morticia shuddered, moaning out loud, yet she had barely a chance to get any words out as a tentacle was shoved into her mouth, grinding into the back of her throat. It was rough and it was coarse – and the tentacle monster most certainly didn't ask for her permission out there in the depths of the plunging, churning ocean. It was good, in that case, that her permission was given in her willing freefall, launching herself out over the edge into the unknown, all to be filled in every hole she had available, again and again.

Her naked scales were caressed and adorned, yet the dragoness anthro no longer had any sense at all of what was up and what was down, twisting and turning, shifting to the side, her leg flung up, pussy exposed. The folds of it could have been succulent and sweet, but the monster was a brute, only concerned with its own pleasure. A tentacle rammed up into her already soaking wet pussy, stretching her open, and she screamed in a wretched shriek that tore itself from her throat as she twisted and writhed, though there was nowhere at all for her to go, with layer upon layer of coiling tentacles slapped around her.

Yes…

Oh, it was everything she could have wanted and more, double penetrated, her maw stretched wide, teeth digging into the roughness of the tentacle as it crudely face fucked her. It was slippery but not smooth under the layer of lubrication and she hissed up from the back of her throat, though the air that rushed forth had nowhere to go. But the tentacle monster did not care, cramming into her brutally, forcing both her pussy and her throat to stretch around him.

"Mmph!"

She cried out, though all she had was a strangled moan for him, trying to arch her back, twist in his grip, though it even had her tail yanked up and out of the way. It seemed that they didn't want to lose her there as much as she yearned for it too, her pussy softly succulent, dripping with her arousal, the tentacle twisting up against her innermost barrier.

Morticia shuddered bodily. Oh, nothing at all was meant to go through there and even the pressure on her cervix made her stomach lurch, though there was something, she could not tell what, in the magic of the tentacle monster that let her barrier, slowly, so slowly, open up around its penetrating push.

And it felt better than ever, the tentacle cramming into every last inch of her body it had available, driving up deep into her womb. For its seed could not go anywhere else, if she was to be filled with their eggs, repeatedly, over and over, until the monster let her go.

Morticia groaned around the tentacle, trying to press her tongue up against it, though she barely had any space in which to wind the slippery appendage around, wanting to pleasure it in a way that the monster had never felt before. Oh, she never wanted to go, leaving her little boat bobbing there as a marker of what had come of her, what she had thrown her body into. Filled and bred, forced to bear clutch after clutch of eggs… The dragoness squirmed and twisted. What more could she ever have wanted, brood mother to a horde of tentacle monsters sent forth to flood the ocean with their lust?

No… No, she never wanted to leave, just to feel her pussy stretch around that thickening tentacle, pumping eggs into her already. With her barrier penetrated and the tentacle driven right up into the back of her womb, there was an easy route into her belly, letting the eggs bulge, one after the other, into her sore and beautifully broken pussy.

Orgasm after orgasm pounded through her, arching her back, twisting her tail into the loving grasp of the tentacles. Never before had it found such a willing partner who tossed themselves into its twisting arms and Morticia was all of that and so much more. Her tail was pinned somewhere against her back, but the dragon was not even aware of the twist in it as another tentacle rammed into her unprotected tail hole. If not for the natural lubrication grinding into her backside, it would have hurt like the blazes, but all she felt was pleasure, shooting her ecstasy into fresh heights.

Three holes… Three tentacles. That shouldn't have left her wanting, but she craved more, needed more, her womb filling up with eggs, one after the other plopping into her. They bulged out through her lower abdomen, and her paws would have gone to them, stroking and caressing, if she had not been as locked into position as she was, howling and climaxing, over and over. There was no escape and yet she ground back passionately on to the tentacles with all her might, slurping down all that lay within her maw, letting it curl down her throat.

There must have been something in the tentacles too that, somehow, allowed her to breathe through them, and she dimly wondered if she would ever need to release them from her lips, forever a breeding vessel, a womb for their eggs to be laid.

Yet there was more, a second tentacle pushing up insistently against the first crammed into her pussy, forcing her body to accept it, inch after inch. She screamed through the bliss of another climax that wasn't hers to take, her womb feeling so large, so full, so strained. Everything was just as she needed it to be, swimming in a haze of lust, her body out of control, her sweet submission guaranteed in all ways.

The tentacle monster's domination was absolute, pounding her, ramming in four tentacles, stretching her pussy beyond all natural limits, its magic making her body softer and more pliable, all so that she could better suit their whims. They had the perfect vessel in her, how she stretched and strained around him, the tentacles pounding, while one swelled with eggs, feeding them straight up into her womb. She had no idea how many had been pumped into her by that point, but she could not find it in herself to care, beyond the need for more, the lust for it, blinking dimly down at her body as her belly inflated as if she was pregnant.

Yes, oh, yes…

So much, so good… Her head drifted, feeling only sensation, barely aware of what she was and what was happening to her. A breeding dragoness for a tentacle monster, as she was, did not have to be at all present in any kind of reality, only there for them, always and forever. Her stomach rumbled as the eggs ground lightly up against one another, bulging out and out until she looked as if she was in the late stages of pregnancy. The rush of water around them in the watery pit of the tentacle monster reminded her of just where she was, though things were not so easy in that regard.

She didn't need to know, drifting, fading, losing her sense of self. All that mattered was her rippling, clenching holes, how she tried to squeeze down around the tentacles as she was ruthlessly pounded, over and over. Her body was there for the monster and only the monster, rumbling a growl, though there was something hotter still seeping into her body, something that even Morticia's lust-addled mind could not understand in the heat of a moment like that.

After all, where eggs were laid, there had to be eggs to seed them too, to fertilise what had been planted. The tentacle monster could more than easily take care of all of that, grinding into her, pounding her deeply, another tentacle questing at her tail hole, though that too was an egg-bearing tentacle. Not every tentacle, after all, had to be for the same purpose, her body opening around them, welcoming them, a slut not on show but kept down there in the dark depths of the ocean like a sordid, dirty secret.

She was their breeding secret, belly larger than it would have been in any pregnancy and bloating out even further still with more and more eggs. They rumbled, her stomach growling, need rising. Her body ached for it, semen creaming and swilling around the eggs in her womb, softening their position, though her belly did not sag at all under the extra weight of it, perfectly supported and bloated luxuriously.

Morticia could not have looked more like a brood mother than she did in that moment, whimpering, moaning, drooling thickly around the tentacle rammed down her throat. She wanted to take more, but, alas, there was a limit to how widely her maw could go, her body aching for more. Her tail hole strained around a second tentacle in her anal ring and she exploded into yet another orgasm at the mere touch of that, five tentacles total slamming into her, using her body like the breeding whore-vessel she had always been meant to be.

Nothing. A whore. A slut. An egg-bearer. That was all that she had ever been meant to be. She had failed in life, worrying about where she had to go, what she had to do, never pursuing her true passions. That was not right, not right in the slightest, her moans rising, flowing through, though they were more muffled still than even they should have been, jaws aching, her body straining, wishing for it all.

Yes… The dragoness was right where she wanted to be, stomach rising, the bulge of eggs rushing into her barely even noticeable anymore. Her pussy stretched wantonly, able to take two eggs inside her body, side by side, at once, though she squealed in climax, toes curling, desperate for even more than she had already been given.

More, yes, always more… She would lust for more, always for more, nothing that the tentacle monster could face her with something that she would turn away from. To be stuffed and filled, suckling desperately on his tentacle for another dose of life-giving seed, pouring down her throat straight into her belly. It was yet another kind of filling and inflation that bulged out her abdomen, another rise forming to smooth out her front, though that creamy load sloshed even more delightfully about in her stomach than it did around the eggs in her womb.

Her mind was no longer hers, not in any significant way, not in any way that mattered anymore. She had given up all of that for the lust of the tentacle monster, the beast that took her, bred her, filled her. In time, she would have to lay the eggs that it had forced up inside her – but could it really be considered forcing when she had dived into the pit of tentacles with such passion and wild abandon?

Her pussy strained, pounded, sore, yet nowhere near being well-bred and filled yet. There was more, the tentacle monster not a creature that had to sleep. They had to have more, to use and abuse her body for the eternity of time, keeping her alive, keeping her wanting – though Morticia was very much already in that state.

All was as it needed to be as the tentacles all writhed inside her at once, the dragoness suckling feverishly around the delicious length grinding between her lips, leaving a sheen of its self-lubrication glistening on them. Yes, yes, she had to please them, all of them, every tentacle with a mind of their own, a sentient being, a monster beyond her wildest dreams and imaginings. Her tail twisted, the tentacles teasing along it and caressing, yet she was exactly where she needed to be, moaning and groaning, every tiny little sensation rising, winding in amongst all the rest.

The swell of her stomach. The strain of her womb. How tight both her pussy and ass were, stuffed with more tentacles than she had ever been stuffed with cock. The push of her tail as she tried to expose her body even more for the monster, all for him, all for her pleasure.

It was all she could do as it rumbled and roared with mindful determination to breed her, tentacles squirming, twisting, pounding her ruthlessly. It was as if everything that they had done to her so far was merely a warm-up, bulges showing through her body as it abused her, a huge swell in her throat heralding the appendage there worming down even more deeply.

Yet the monster climaxing was all she needed, washing down the eggs in seed, roaring, belting out their pleasure above all else. She cried out, though there was no one down there that wanted to hear her cries, whimpering, whining, begging for more with every soundless murmur that managed to pass her lips. Her burning pussy begged for more, her tail hole hungered for it, the pushing force, the ramming power. Her body was to be used, pounded, abused, and only time would tell how many tentacles she could take inside her, all at once, for she would never find her hunger was truly satisfied.

Not as her climax rolled forth, blistering ecstasy pouring through, one orgasm after the other making her whole body tremble as her stomach bloated out larger than she was with a thick deluge of cum. Perfect for a dragoness like her, a breeding vessel, lost to the world and making it so that the tentacle monster would never have to wait and hunger for a single victim more.

She needed it. Needed them. Just as they needed her.

She groaned, delirious with lust. Time no longer had any meaning, her body swollen, the fetish of it all finally becoming her blissful reality. Inside her gut, the eggs shifted softly against one another, suitably cradled in a bath of cum, fertilised. Though they would not be ready to be laid for at least a month yet.

Until then, she would carry them. Only to be impregnated with eggs over and over again. Morticia shivered, though not from cold.

Her life was finally complete, her body a breeder's heaven. There was no more that she could have ever wanted.

Trapped by the Tentacles

I knew what I was doing but that did not make it right to venture into the countryside – well, far beyond that now. I needed to get into the backwoods, the depths of English forest where the undergrowth was thick and I swore and cursed and hacked my way through, scratching up my arms and legs as I fought for what I deserved. My nails were ruined but I'd only had the manicure done for a wedding anyway and didn't often care for things like that, although my hair too still held a little of the fine oils and gels, potions and lotions that I wouldn't usually spend money on myself. I never saw the point of things like that when it would all become ruined and smudged and wasted in the throes of lust.

That was what I, Mattie, wanted the most out of life. Career and family be damned – I didn't need someone to stay with me for life when I could seek out kinky lusts over and over again on my own or with friends who had become my family. Heavily into BDSM and exploring every last nuance of the scene, I was a wolfess in the prime of her life that loved everything to do with it, although nothing really sat for long with me as I changed the colour of my long hair, down to the middle of my back, to match my personality, forcing those around me to keep up.

"Here?"

I paused before the wall, although it looked like nothing, a crumbling ruin draped in ivy and moss, something that the land itself was set on reclaiming. And yet this strange wall set out in the middle of nowhere, thick forest surrounding me, was the key to something that I had not yet had the luxury of experiencing for myself, lips pressed together even though I could not truly seal my passion behind them. My ears twitched, tail lifted, though tucking it down in trepidation may have been more accurate for me.

Oh, I wanted it. And I would find the entrance they spoke of.

It should not have come together so easily for me but I found the hole; the old tunnel that could have been a mine shaft if it had been anywhere else but was a pathway into the bowels of a castle that had, in its prime, held so many secrets. No one said it was true but there were some that spoke of it with a gleam in their eyes that, well, had made me think, originally, that there was a little something more to those kinky tales than I may have otherwise put stock in.

Now was the time for truth and I flashed the torch back and forth, wishing that I had my old, comfortable hiking boots with me. My new ones pinched my toes but I had to press on, clothes tight in the wrong places along with the right ones, but I had to keep going, following the beam of the torch as the temperature dropped beneath the ground, tugging my jacket closer around my torso and shoulders.

A rumble... Was that something more? Water streamed down the walls but disappeared deeper without forming something that I needed to either step through or over, chest heaving as I struggled for breath. I had to be strong, had to be brave, had to keep pushing on. Above all else, regardless of my fear shivering at my hackles, I had to find out the truth. It could be the key to everything that I had been seeking for so long.

The tunnel opened out and then I saw it – but I did not dare lay eyes on it for too long! It? Was that the right term of address? Probably not, but I could not speak that allowed, dropping to my knees and throwing myself down before what I had sought out, lips parted in a moan and my pussy, well... I couldn't think too much about what that part of my anatomy was doing, lest I lose control entirely and rip my clothes off right then and there. I did shrug my furred body out of my jacket, wanting something at least to cover me up as I left myself there, prostrated, a helpless victim of a greater being that, if the rumours were true, needed me and my essence as much as I needed them.

It could be false. But I had to try, had to try my best in the beam of the torch, the glow flickering as if it would peter out, illuminating the plant-like being that could be the key to unlocking so much that I had not even dared to imagine. And yet I had to believe in it too, they said, or it just wouldn't work, which forced me to suspend my belief and disbelief of what reality could and could not be more than I could ever have imagined.

"My lord... I have come."

I did not know what would happen, but I stayed there, less than patiently, with my head bowed, the only mark of respect that I knew how to give, muzzle dipped quietly. There, I waited, lingering and waiting and hoping and waiting as if I had nothing better in the world to do, wishing for something more even though I still didn't know if I was being made a fool of or not. But what I so desperately needed was to know either way and I had to try, try and then try again, harder still, to come to the realisation of the life that I was meant to have, one way or another.

Something slimy brushed my ankle and I gasped, head shooting up, hair falling across my line of sight at the moment that I truly needed to see what was going on. Black shaded my view and the torch spun, shadows jagged and monstrous on the wall – yet the monster of beauty before me was what I truly wanted to see, the writhing mass of seductive tentacles that could have simply belonged to a plant but truly belonged to so very much more than that. Twisting and turning amongst one another, they were all part of one being, although I could not see them in their entirety, glimpses swelling into the torchlight and disappearing again as quickly as they had appeared.

Speed was the name of the tentacle monster's game and I squealed as I was hauled up by my ankle, dangled upside down with so many tentacles, all shapes and sizes, lunging for me. Some were thicker than the others and they wrapped around my waist and shoulders, supporting me in mid-air, while others spread my legs, squirmed up beneath my clothes to rip them from my fur. Just like that, it no longer mattered what I had or hadn't worn that day, rendered completely naked with even my shoes yanked off, bare toes curling in the raw essence of vulnerability.

It was almost shameful how wet I was but I could not help but press into those tentacles, cry out for their embrace, one sliding tantalisingly across my darker, wolf-ish lips. I captured it there in the warmest, wettest kiss I possibly deliver, suckling and teasing, my tongue demonstrating every last trick in its extensive repertoire, curling and flicking and licking along the tentacle that so graced me with its attention. The monster shuddered against me and, heart pounding, I took that to mean that they enjoyed it, redoubling my efforts and sloppily blowing the tentacle as if it was a cock even as the tip of it thickened and flared and…

…exploded in my mouth! My eyes shot wide but there was nothing to see but a shifting, twisting mass in the darkness, what could only be cum flowing urgently into the back of my mouth. I gulped it down automatically, not willing to let a single drop of it go to waste, something flowery and thick flooding my nostrils, infiltrating my system as that sweeter not saltier taste brought me solidly back to the reality of it all, a reckless laugh trying to bubble up from my throat. Maybe it would have been successful too if my mouth had not been stuffed full of tentacle-dick but I wouldn't have wanted it any other way as the tentacles spun me and flipped me, crawling up the insides of my thighs with ruthlessly lustful intent.

They wanted something and I drank down that cum as they sank into my pussy, two slender tentacles together, squirming and worming their way deeper and deeper as my muffled moans filled the chamber. My heart leapt and pounded and I could hardly breathe but I was right where I wanted to be in the breath of the moment, eyes closed and the world around me spinning and spinning with heated lust, never to come to any kind of end. The stretch between my legs was immense and I had to yank my thighs out wider still to maintain it, heaving and puffing, eyes darting even beneath lowered lids.

Hold out… I just had to hold out, the twinge of pain swiftly fading to ridiculous pleasure – pleasure that one wolf's body should never have been able to contain for itself. And yet I had to, all for the lust that had brought me there in the first place, passion driving me on to hump and grind back against those rampantly thrusting tentacles, begging them on and on and on to power into my wanton pussy, stretching it out more than it ever had before. Something wet flowed down my legs and I realised with a start that they too were ejaculating inside me, a flood of cum that was far too much for my pussy to hold seeping out, even as they strove to ram up into my cervix, a painful twist in my guts.

They would have all they wanted from me, however, as I was restrained in living, changing bondage, moaning and grunting and arching my back, begging for more in all the ways that I possibly could without words. Yes, oh, yes! I wanted it all, wanted them to give it to me, those tentacles in my cunt swapping for another thicker one that made me groan louder than ever, begging for it. I was nothing more than a slut for them, twisting and groaning and begging for all they dared give me, hips working as they hammered in harder than any man. Oh, who could have had a male after such an experience of being filled, strained and stretched to the edge of my limits and then pushed beyond even that too?

They had more in mind for me though, squeezing up between my butt for the pucker of that hole too, a slimed-up tentacle questing for entry that I willingly allowed. That did not stop my body from clenching down around it in raw joy though as I squealed and tried to kick, to jerk in ecstasy, balanced on the brink of an orgasm that very nearly felt as if it would completely and utterly overwhelm me.

And yet I had to hold it back, had to hold in my joy, letting orgasm power through and through me, my whole body rising and undulating passionately on a sea of tentacles from which I wanted no release. They could have me forever, if they wanted, my heart flowing along with the twist of them, desire curling up inside as my pussy clenched and twitched erratically, lacking muscular control in climax, orgasm powering on and on, something that could not be denied as much as I may otherwise have wanted to hold it close to my heart for just a little while longer.

They did not tire as I did, sending cum down my throat by means of providing sustenance, although I was only too glad to drink it down gladly. It was sweeter than juice and coming with the sort of flavour that could be found in the tropics, leading one to question where it was something to drink or something to eat, the confused line flitting between the two.

Running my longer, more flexible tongue lovingly along a tentacle with a defined, cock-like head with glands, I growled out my pleasure, hair clinging to the fur of my neck where so much of their slime and self-lubrication had glazed my skin. Every inch of me was soaked with their lust and juices and there was nothing at all that I would have wanted to change about that as I arched and moaned, rocked and turned and twisted on ever-flowing, wanton ecstasy.

My anal ring, however, was not used to such a stretch and they forced it to strain wider and wider still into a lewd gape that seemed as if it would not be able to close up again even after our furtively seductive tryst in the darkness was good and done. I groaned and clenched my teeth but they stroked and supported my head, brushing my lips as if in a kiss to encourage me on, letting me know that I could take it, if only I relaxed. I had to listen to them, had to trust them, had to push on through past the limit of what I thought could not be possible, my pussy pounded and soaked, a mixture of my juices and their cum flowing from me, spurting and sloshing out messily. Their ejaculate soaked my thighs, sinking into my fur and marking me as theirs, the reek of them swelling through my lungs as I took each shuddering breath.

Every last bit of me was a hot mess and I panted out another orgasm, hardly finding the breath for that while all I wanted to do, so very desperately, was to throw my head back and *scream*. For they had so much more to give me and I knew that as a deliciously knobbly, *huge* tentacle was forced into my cunt, forcing my body to accept it as I consented to the rough, passionate sex with every moan that passed my sweetly parted lips.

There was no sense of time down there, only darkness, the torch static where it had been dropped and rendering monstrously erotic images in the shadows on the wall. Tentacles breaking free, one plunging to my mouth, the shape of my head cast in stark definition in the moment before the monster and I became one again, my holes pounded, filled in every orifice that I could ever have dreamed of having. The tentacles in my pussy and anal passage squeezed up against one another and it was hard to tell where one orgasm ended and the next began, cast and writhing on a never-ending sea of ecstasy that had no beginning and no true end either.

Not that I wanted it to end, of course, as the tentacles pulled back from my muzzle, lining up to take their best shots, a storm of cock-tips wanting my attention. And I gave it all to them readily and willingly, my lips parted like a seductress, a sexy whore, in a pornographic film watched under the cover of darkness, something so racy that she would have… Well, no, I would have shared any manner of porn with a lover, all for the sake of our pleasure, but the meaning was still there!

I wanted it all and I spread my arms out, hardly restrained at all, more supported so that the tentacles did not send me flying to the floor, my body contorting beautifully, imagining myself to be a goddess of lust in the moment. I was more than I had ever been as a human and the world, the tentacle monster, needed to see that as I moaned and took their loads across my face, far more than a mere pearl necklace staining me. Thick rivers of cum ran down my face and I lapped it saucily off my hands, sucking it off my fingers, although I had no eyes to maintain contact with. The monster got the gist of what I was doing, seemingly, and shivered again, doubling down on the thrusts into my pussy, tightening up even as they sought to strain me open into a gaping hole of lust that could never again close up.

Maybe that was all I needed to be, I thought as

cum shot across my body, my face, my hair. They took me like the tentacle monster's whore I truly was and I relished in it, moaning for more, suckling every tentacle offered up to my lips and letting them seed me, mark me as their own. I didn't have to be something or someone other than who I was, just the bitch of a monster intent on breeding me over and over again, and I lusted after that simple sense of reality when reality itself had seemed dull and lonesome in the days before the tentacle monster had come into my life, even if I had been the one to seek him out.

My most powerful orgasm yet hit me then and the tentacles went crazy, pounding and writhing, hammering and slamming into me with the force of a being possessed, spinning through lust even in the cloak of darkness. Still, even there, I was stripped bare of who I had been, born anew in the slimy embrace of one who could reveal who I was better than I even knew myself.

Rocking in the arms of the tentacles, my encounter was not to end anytime soon. And that was just the way I wanted it to be, heaving and panting for more, a creature reduced to sexual lust alone that could not be sated by anything else ever again. No… I would always need the tentacle monster to bring me off going forward, our fates intertwined. I only hoped as they spent their umpteenth load into me that they would want me back too as much as I wanted to be there, moaning and begging them to give me all they had and so much more too.

Sucking in a breath, I screamed in orgasm, breasts trembling. It was all as it was meant to be, all at long last, and I relished each and every tiny, lingering sensation.

It was mine, all mine.

And I would never be without the lure of that

ecstasy again.

Lustful Experimentation

Stacey groaned, the sound rising up from the back of her throat even though it did not seem to go anywhere. She knew where she was but not right at that time, floating and twisting and turning in a chamber that wrapped sweetly around her, lifting her up and wavering her on the line between reality and fantasy. And yet she had become all too aware during recent weeks that that line could be blurred so very easily, unknowing of what was awaiting her this time in the kinky, sexual experiments that she had been keen to sign up for.

Ah... She'd been so innocent when she'd signed the release forms but it could not have been better, her world changed forever. Her long, black hair fanned out around her and she smiled, although there was no one there to bear witness to it. Whether she was lying down or not did not matter to her as she parted her lips, face devoid of make-up...

Down and down and down... The world simmered away around her into pure blackness, yet the sensation of cloth draping and dragging over her body remained. Where was she? Or, more accurately, where was she going? She would soon see and Stacey cried out as she landed, a pit forming around her, the sky so very far above that the square of light that it graced her with may as well have not existed at all.

"Hello?"

Little one...

The voice sinuously snaked its way into her mind and the tentacles of the beast were wrapped around her ankles, tipping her away from the light, although it was not as if she would have been making any kind of escape towards it anyway. That was not for Stacey as she squealed and let the tentacles lift her, dangling in the air as the earth walls of the pit blocked out her line of sight, everything simmering down to sweet sensation. But that was alright too, what she needed, the crawl of the slimy tentacles easing up her thighs, spreading them wide as her breath caught, eyes scanning and scanning and scanning and only seeing a twisting, writhing mass.

It was quick this time! He, it – the pronoun didn't matter – wasn't hanging around as they clutched her up, finding teases that she could not have imagined before, her nipples perking up to a touch that was hotter than any human. But it was all in the machine, the mental stimulation firing off – or was it? She never could quite tell what the climax machine was researching, besides getting off, and she wasn't about to complain all that loudly either if it meant she got what she needed too, over and over again, from its kinky embrace.

The monster twisted around her and Stacey could not help but lean into it, letting it heft up her legs as she lost sense of which way was up and which way was down, whimpering into its lustful hold. It twisted and squeezed and she cried out for it, the tip of a tentacle, slithering and green, nearly black, grazing her throbbing bud of a clit, pussy shaven softly bare for the sexy occasion. Well, she wouldn't have wanted to disappoint her suitor, after all, would she?

Not your cunt...

No, this beast wanted something far more deliriously passionate from her as she moaned and arched in its grasp, giving herself over to the monster that the climax chamber had sent to her this day. Whether it was fantasy or reality still remained to be seen but Stacey was more than happy to go along with it, leaning into the brush of tentacles as they squirmed their way up her body, wrapping around her breasts and squeezing deliciously. The tentacles could lubricate themselves (apparently) and she could not have honestly said she was surprised as it teased up against the bud of her forbidden entrance, the pucker closing and clenching tightly as if to keep it out. Yet Stacey had no such desire to deny either the tentacle monster of the simulation climax chamber or herself that pleasure as she opened up to him, allowing him to plunge the slick appendage deep up past the barrier of her anal ring.

And what kind of barrier was it, really, to be put in place against a higher form of pleasure altogether? Stacey groaned and panted, her mouth open so wide that it felt as if her tongue was pushing out over her lips, although she was not a dog or anything like that by any means, something that could fall prey to baser instincts when they should have been proud and dominant, the top of the food chain. Human beings could be so complacent in their power that they too forgot to submit and that was exactly what she did as the kinky tentacle monster wormed its way deeper and deeper into her anal passage, curling up deeply against her most sensitive places.

Well, all of her spots in there were sensitive but it knew just how to make her squirm, toes curling and flexing, head swimming pleasantly as she moaned and twisted, arching her back for more: always, *more*.

It was obliging – oh, how it was – pushing a second tentacle into her anal ring, so big that it was a wonder it even fit at all. The strain was immense and she nearly climaxed right then and there from that stimulation alone, panting so heavily that it proved a strain on her aching lungs to snatch every hard-won breath. Stacey heaved, eyes wide, but that wasn't going to help her as she whined and twisted, tentacles crawling over her like snakes as each and every one of them left a slickly slimy trail behind, coating her in the ooze that both teased and provided her holes with such an ample amount of lubrication.

It was not only her backdoor entrance that was destined to undergo such pleasure, however, as another tentacle shot into her pussy, scoring a direct hit as it drove smoothly all the way up to her cervix without hitting it – now that was a discomfort that was not pleasant for any woman! Her inner walls closed down softly around it, trying to squeeze, and yet the girth of the tentacle was too meaty for her to push all that hard against it, a delicious stretch that strained through her pussy into her anal passage, all tentacles seemingly trying to cram up against one another.

Her head swam, struggling to keep her grip on reality. Yet what even was reality anymore? What was her sense of self, her sense of being? Who was she? Just a sex toy for a monster? That was all she needed to be, lips parted and gasping, hankering for something other than breath.

"Please... *Please*!"

The good thing about where she was meant that she didn't have to worry about getting all her words out in time: his tentacle drove between her lips regardless. He knew what he needed from her and what she needed from him, supplying it in heady, ample doses, more than any one human could take, really. But the shot of cum that poured down her throat was everything that she could have ever asked for and more, her throat working to gulp it down, every last drop. Like a guy's cock crammed up into the back of her throat, on the edge of making her heave for breath and resisting the urge to gag, it creamed into her mouth, pouring and flooding, the delicious treat that she'd wanted all along.

Of course, the tentacles had the added effect of being able to suppress her gag reflex and she parted her lips even more, willingly trusting them to slither down her throat, claiming her entirely. They could pull back to allow her breath but her head pounded with the control they took from her, desire rising up as her pussy clenched down on the tentacle in her cunt, wanting more and more and more. But nothing could stop the rise of orgasm curling up within her, exploding and claiming her body, taking it from her hold as she whimpered and whined, although not even Stacey herself could be sure whether she was making any noise or not.

All that mattered was that driving pulse, coming with a flow and nothing of an ebb, her holes pounding, mouth full of a tentacle-cock. Breath was only allowed when the monster snarled and allowed it to be so but that was by the by as she sacrificed control in lieu of pleasure, the howling throb of ecstasy rocking her, twisting... Was she upside down? Stacey groaned and tried to rock her hips but the tentacles held her so tightly that she couldn't even turn, let alone breathe freely. Yet she wanted to be moaning, submissive to the nth degree, lost to the world. She didn't have to think, have to control, all she had to do was be in the moment and the tentacles, those divine pleasure-givers, would give the rest of it to her.

And there were more tentacles too, tiny ones that suctioned their little 'mouths' around her nipples, sucking and pulling, although she had no milk to give them that time. Maybe she could visit the monster again when she was lactating? Well, she wasn't in control of what happened in the climax chamber but maybe she could suggest it, if she even remembered the passing thought when she left, tentacles slithering over her, a slimy mass that was forever changing.

Nothing was the same and nothing was stable as she moaned and arched and rocked and groaned, sounds coming from her that should never have been born from human lips. She was otherworldly, a seductress who could defeat anything and anyone one – well, as long as it involved her sexual prowess, that was. Stacey was invincible and all she needed was one more orgasm as her backside was pounded, the tentacles growing to colossal proportions inside her. Surely there was no possible way that those could fit inside her and yet her passion needed to come through, moaning and slurping along with one that was so very lovingly pounding her mouth and throat as if it was the last thing in the world that would ever linger of any sexual experience of hers.

The tentacles pulled and tugged at her nipples, larger tentacles squeezing and massaging her breasts. The massage was far better than anything she could ever have taken from a human, whether she had lain with a man or a woman. She arched into it, pushing her chest out at an angle that spoke entirely of her lust, the tentacle in her mouth ripping itself free just in the nick of time. And that was not because it wanted to call halt to any manner of the proceedings at all but something else entirely, a jet of cum pouring over her face and hair as if it was coming from a fountain.

Drinking from the tap, she whined and opened her mouth wide for the deluge, wanting to taste every drop that the monster was kind enough to expend, tentacles propping her head up very kindly so that she could take it all. It spattered her face, giving her beautifully naked body far more than a pearl necklace, soaking her hair and dripping down her neck – and yet she loved every moment of it. It was where she was supposed to be and she cried out for more, another orgasm lingering on the edges of her mind, desperate to rise and take her again from reality into undulating passion.

But that was not all that could come for her and her world twisted and turned all over again as she whimpered, lips slick with cum and her anal ring aching pleasantly. There was not a single jot of pain in her mind as those tentacles fattened up and she moaned to see the bulges travelling down the length of them, moving more and more quickly to the helpless holes of her anal passage and pussy. There was no going back and, despite what her body could naturally hold, the tentacle monster was going to have her well and truly one way or another.

Cum spurted into her and the monster trembled, every tentacle shuddering as if it too was experiencing pleasure from the liaison. Of course, he was but she could not ask him that as cum flooded her, oozing out of her holes even as it strained her, pumping in more and more relentlessly. They did not pull out and her stomach swelled grossly, pushing out and out and out as so much cum, more than she could hold, was rammed in, forced deep up inside her, where it was meant to be.

In her mind, as the tentacles tugged and pulled and *licked* at her nipples, she would become pregnant from the tentacle monster, those many, many little sperms racing for her eggs, seeding a clutch that she would then, later, have to lay. Whether or not the eggs would be viable was another question entirely, but she did not care, her mind swirling and taken up by the thought of squatting, maybe even pushing out those eggs while the monster fucked her ass...

Yes, yes, that would do nicely! Oh, she needed it! She needed it so badly! And she took every drop of cum that the monster poured into her, pumping and filling her up beyond all natural measures, swelling and swelling. She didn't want to look down but the tentacles had to shift and writhe to better cup and cradle her belly, raising her up so that she was so high that she could have possibly gotten out of the pit, trembling and throbbing, her whole body on fire.

Every nerve-ending in her body fired off as cum spurted and drooled from her in thick, fat globules, staining her inner thighs and buttocks, every inch of her either covered in slime or semen. There was nothing more that she could do or say to get what she needed, forced to both linger and languish, one sensation overwhelming the next as strain overcame her body.

They snaked over her and she moaned as her snatch was plundered, although it didn't even feel like hers anymore, how sweetly it clenched and squeezed. And yet the strangeness too was welcome in the way that it made her groan, rocking and twisting, the tentacles rotating within her as if they too were intent on trying to drive up something more from their slinky, kinky interlude. They'd have it all again, she was sure, milking and squeezing her tits as she rocked into another orgasm, moaning open-mouthed as cum flowed into it, her pink lips parted for the gift it offered her, willing to drink down more and more even as her stomach rose grossly and shockingly distended.

It was all she needed and all they deserved, together, taking that ecstasy from the climax chamber, tentacles crawling over her, owning her. Stacey would not have wanted to be anywhere else if she'd been given a second choice or chance, kissing and suckling whatever tentacles her lips touched, legs lewdly spread as she was laid flat, a seething bed of plant-matter holding her sweetly steady.

And yet she could not stay there in the fantasy forever, the monster laying her down with the tentacles still around her, squeezing and caressing, teasing her without wriggling free. But there was nothing that could be done for the slipping away of the dream even as she whimpered and clawed for it, letting the afterglow take her, however much she wanted to stay.

The in-between world took her in cooling arms, simmering down her lust and passion; as much as she wanted to stay there, there always had to be a sense of respite at some point. To recover meant that she could return more quickly, assisting with the research of the climax chamber and all the fantasies that could be played out there over and over again. Some would say that there was no end and there was no end to it all that Stacey had found yet. To keep trying was to keep living and she rolled in the sweet caress of darkness, swimming and floating and rising back to a world that called her with sugar-sweet tones.

Coming around in the climax chamber, she awoke lying on a padded bed of sorts, although it would not have been the type that one would have retreated to on a late night. The breaks in the bed allowed for it to be positioned with the person's head high or low, a bend in their legs or even an arch in their back, all with the manner of comfort in mind. Whether she had fallen into the simulation from that seat or not was not something that she recalled and neither did it matter as the technician monitoring the screens beside her, wires hooked up to her bare skin, working away.

"Was it a pleasant experience?" The technician said, studiously not looking at her as he monitored the machines beside her bed, even though her body was covered by a sheet. "The data this time was...interesting."

Too late, he realised that he had not been meant to say that, but Stacey was too far gone to complain, grinning widely as she sat up, the sheet clutched, surprisingly, demurely to her chest. Her eyes gleamed and she could hardly stop herself from moaning, inner thighs soaked and legs pressed together, desperate for more already as she implored him with the shining orbs of her eyes alone, hair clinging down with light static.

"When can we run that simulation again?"

It was going to prove to be a highly successful experiment in record time.

Bound Luxury

Nessa flew slowly, languidly, almost as if the quadrupedal dragoness was trying to be caught. The trees bristled with life before her, of the deciduous fare, but they were not the sort of foliage that one should have ventured close to, knowing what they were. Yet her green scales bristled with a delight that only she knew of, flying lower and lower, until the lighter plate-scales of her stomach brushed the tree-tops, rustling through.

The vine shot out before she had a chance to react and yet it was with a delighted squeal that her form plunged through the leaves, ignoring the scrape of branches on her hide. The thick vine tightened its grip around the base of her tail, dragging her backwards without a care for her comfort. But that was just what Nessa wanted, cool shade slipping over her, crashing into the ground even though it was not much of a bump at all, for the vines held her fast, more and more lashing out, wrapping around her legs, even the base of her wings. They weren't about to let her go in a hurry and she relished in the restriction, a low whimper breaking the barrier of her narrow lips, though the moisture within would not linger for long with such passion in the air.

She wanted it, wanted everything that the vines had for her as they twisted up around her body, trussing her up delightfully in a way that she yearned for, whimpering out loud. Nessa's cries would not be heard by anyone, however, but that was just how she wanted it as sunset lit up the top side of the forest, leaving her in the delicious shade beneath, cooling her scales. The vines dragged her deep, though the moss was soft and gentle enough on her stomach to not cause her any real issues. She could kick her legs back as her heart pounded, wings strapped to her body by the vines that promised so much pleasure, if only she had the strength of heart and presence in mind to give in to it.

Down into a cave she was dragged, passive and limp even with her moans already rising. She wanted to both be present in the moment so that she could feel every last little thing happening to her and yet…she didn't want to be an active player in it. The vines acted more stringently than the tighter bondage while still being able to reposition her at a moment's notice, just so that they could place her exactly where they wanted her. There was nothing complicated in the smooth slide of plant-material, a distinctly different sensation to flesh or scales, over her body, yet she could still just about glimpse the dropping light of the outside world as they finally stilled.

Well, she stilled, breathing heavily, eyes wide, her neck wrapped up in vines so that she could not even twist her head back and forth. Nessa groaned deep in the back of her throat and would have lifted her tail for the slithering encroach of vines if they had not already yanked it up out of the way, bowed over her back as if to ensure that her exposure was one that was irreversible. The dragoness shuddered and whimpered and yet it was all in the name of more, lusting for the vines so terribly that she doubted that she would have at all been able to take what she needed from them if she had, indeed, been free to do so for herself.

No, she needed to be restrained, to feel the delicious pull of them on her scales, restricting her and placing her body and limbs just where they needed to be. The vines were curious beings, however rough they were in snatching their "prey" out of the skies and the surrounding forest, and she whimpered softly as they tickled her lips. It was a breath of a kiss that she could only welcome, two sliding in at once and easing in the back of her throat, demanding entrance with such a light touch that her body could not help but to give it. Instantly, her body reacted to the sap coated them, slickening their plant-flesh as if it was something else entirely and numbing her throat. One of the vines tickled all the way down into her lungs, following the path of her windpipe, and took over breathing for her, feeding air down and expelling waste as if it was as natural as, well, breathing to her.

She wouldn't need the vines out of her mouth until they were good and done with her, she thought through a haze of, as yet, unfulfilled lust, trying to wriggle her hips, to encourage them to do as they willed with her. It was all that Nessa wanted and yet the ability to gain it for herself had, in effect, been stripped from her, need pounding through, a driving force clawing at the back of her mind that had to be paid tribute and testament to. The slit under her tail that held both her anal passage and her feminine one was flushed and drooling already with her juices, the glisten of them tempting, so very tempting.

The vines could not resist, curling around her tail and delving in, though they were not only after the breeding portion of her body. As Nessa squealed and tried to writhe in absolute bliss, a thick vine slammed into her tail hole too, cramming into the stretched slit of her draconian cloaca, stretching her out and spreading her open without any care for her comfort. Still, she opened up readily enough around the both of them, their slick pumping filling her delightfully, her cunny clenching around the vine as if to drag it deeper even then when she should have been allowing her body to relax and accept it.

Nessa's head swum as if she had been flying at too high of an altitude for even a dragon for too long, her tail tip curling back and forth, just about the only part of her body that was longer permitted to move. Her throat bulged around the two tentacles rammed in there and her eyes watered, striving to see what was right there before her muzzle, even though that in itself seemed more difficult in the moment. She was strung out and splayed across the soft dirt of the cave floor and yet even the grit of it ground into her scales, dirtying her as if she was not worth keeping clean even for the pleasure of the breeding plant.

For Nessa more than knew what the vines had in store for her as they pumped her full, one even managing to, gently, tease up into her womb, the secretions oozing forth to soften any defences that her body may have instinctually put in place. She just wanted them deeper, curling up into her womb, spilling their seed forth, the cool flow of it splashing out as if the plants intended on filling her until she popped. Nessa groaned, panting heavily through the breathing-tube of a vine, eyes half-closed, languishing in pleasure.

So full...

Yet if she thought she was full then things were going to change very quickly for her as the vines progressed, pumping and grinding like the best cocks that she could ever have imagined, yet their thickness stretched her out more than any drake. Another overly eager vine- tentacle joined her in her pussy, straining her tight passage to what may have felt like her breaking point, if she had not already been ready and wanting for them, striving to grind back even then. The restrictions tightened, locking her in place, stretching one of her legs out a little further, all to simply remind her of her place. And her place was to remain there, bred and ready for more, until the breeding-plant had no further use for her.

The flow of seed poured forth without a spurt to break it up, an unstoppable flow, though it took her a moment longer to realise that it was flowing up under her tail too, into her backdoor entrance. Moaning, she tried to twist without thinking about it, muscles aching, the delicious lines of tension lacing her body driving her on. Why being restricted felt so good, powerless in the moment, she would never know but that was not something Nessa had to bear in mind as the tentacles thickened.

Not all at once though, not all the way down the length: in bulges. The eggs travelled down slowly, following the last of the stream of seed, for the monster-plant did not need to use her eggs to use her as a breeding vessel, something to be laid into and no more than that. All that mattered was that her body was ripe to be used as a holding ground for its eggs, the plant caring no more for her than that. Her flanks bulged out before her hind legs, fattening and thickening with the eggs as they plopped into the pool of seed, the neck of her womb straining to accept them. Any pain that came with it was fleeting and lost anyway in her muffled "glark" of orgasm, crying out around the vines as they stuffed both her maw and throat full.

Oh, they thrust and thrust, all of the vines all at once, and yet she knew none of that, carried to a blissful high in their arms. They held and caressed her, rippling over her scales without reducing the restriction of her bondage one bit in the course of it, her pants coming more and more headily, yet she never the once struggled to get all the breath she needed into her lungs. No, the plants took care of that, the vines slurping up and absorbing her juices even as she climaxed, head spinning and spinning, devious delight taking over.

All she could do was to ride it out as more and more eggs plopped into her, though she had not bothered to keep count of them. The pace, however, felt more urgent than before and she squirmed delightedly, one climax pulsing into the next as they forced their way through the welcoming grip of her pussy, funnelling them up into her womb and her backdoor passage too. Her tail-star, tucked in her cloaca, strained around them, the widest object that had ever passed up there, and she cried out in bliss, rocked through orgasm after orgasm as her flanks could not help but bulge.

They cared not for her, only for filling her with their eggs. A pause between batches of laying allowed the vines to deposit more seed into her, washing down the eggs as her stomach bloated out heavily, giving her the impression that, indeed, she was already pregnant. The majority of what was in her guts and womb, however, was the seed of the plant, keen to ensure that every last one of its eggs came to sweet fruition, fertilised within her. It was not all that often that a breeding-plant like them found a willing host and they were something to both be cherished and coveted with the wicked intelligence curling through the vines, delighting in breeding joy.

They pounded her deep, driving a muffled snarl from her muzzle, barely even realising that the vines had flipped her up into the air so that she hung there, suspended, whimpering where she was. It opened up her belly to even more filling, the eggs pumped into her anal passage working their way back up through her body, for there was only one place that they could go as her stomach inflated out with them. She whimpered and twisted, head spinning lightly, yet it was rare that pleasure actually threatened to overwhelm her.

Nessa swore that her scales squeaked and groaned as her hide was forced to stretch more and more, straining to contain the bulging mass of eggs within her. Their soft shells pressed up wantonly against one another almost as if they were trying to merge but not even they were able to do that as the vine moved amongst them in her womb, adjusting and shifting their position so that they rested in the best way to grow within her.

The dragoness heaved and panted, her belly sagging heavily as the weight within it ballooned. Inflation could be lightening but there was a certain kind of weight to bearing eggs that were not her own to carry, tail swinging faintly, the vines shifting once again. They eased over her, setting her back legs on the ground, though that was only for Nessa to balance, the rolling sag of her rounded-out stomach drawing the most attention. Not even the vines could leave it alone as she trembled under their touch, how they crawled over her scales, the rise of her belly a little on the lumpy side considering just how many eggs had already been forced into her.

But there were more, so many more, a gush of seed heralding the encroach of more, orgasm tickling at the back of her mind. Nothing was under the dragoness' control and she whined mutely around the vines, lashing them with her tongue, though that only made them squirm and bulge into her throat all the more. Emboldened, she did it again, though the fit of them in her maw was too tight for much flexibility there, the vines squirming and wriggling, thrusting maniacally. Any pleasure taken there would render her a little sore afterwards but not incapacitated in any way, though she would remember them fondly when her belly was fat and full of eggs simply waiting to be laid – for a second time.

Losing sense of reality, her belly sagged heavily, bloating out and out, the eggs pushing up against one another urgently within as the vines spent another load. It evened out the otherwise lumpy swell of her stomach a little more and yet was still not quite enough to ease the tension in her scales, stretched taut and bulging as if she was going to pop right there and then. She whimpered and tried to rock her hips back and forth but even that minute motion was denied to her, need coursing through, on the edge of another orgasm. That was for the final and largest batch of eggs, however, her body aching and twitching around the vines as lump after lump of egg travelled down the length of the impregnating tendrils.

It felt wrong to have them pushed up into her stomach, but the rising swell of it was what sent her screaming mutely over the edge, twisting and writhing to the extent that the vines allowed, though they were most likely thrusting too wildly to care. All she cared about was her pleasure, letting it go on and on and on, rippling through her in waves and pulses that she hoped would never end. She needed it, egg after egg disappearing into her, her stomach round with them, the round of her womb inflating melding slowly with that of her actual stomach, a thick rise of dragon-flesh that contained new life.

The vines thrust and thrust, knowing only to keep going until their job was done. but that end was something that could only be delivered with one, final burst of seed, the dragoness' stomach almost as large as the bulk of her body with eggs and seed, groaning with the weight of it. The last dousing of seed painted the eggs, the vine squirming within her cervix – a strange sensation that could have been uncomfortable (if not, of course, outright painful) if not for the numbing sap. As it was, the tingling pleasure that it brought instead had her moaning and striving to hump her hips, to get even more in her, caught up in the delirium of pleasure.

Time passing lost all meaning as the eve of the day closed out at the cave mouth, though she was left in the arms of the vines, wrapped up and resting there without a care, slipping down to her side. Her neck still bulged with the might of the vines but Nessa had no concern about being able to breathe with the breathing tube still inserted, as sore as her throat was from their presence. Relaxation of that part of her would come in time and she gratefully murred around the length of the vines as they released a little more sap all over again, soothing away any aches that may have occurred there.

So thoughtful…

Yet all that the dragoness could think about was how round her stomach was, so very many eggs, all smaller than a dragon-egg and still sizeable, delivered into her holes. Her anal ring tightened around the vines but she had no wish to see them removed, softening in her lust even as her body begged for rest. The vines knew how to keep a victim there for as long as possible and must have felt something more in her that could be put to use, keeping her there rather than merely releasing her and letting her waddle off with a fat belly full of their eggs and essence.

Seed trickled from her, a tickling ooze around the vines, and she closed her eyes, breathing slowly and evenly through the tube, the plant even controlling her breathing for her. There was nothing to worry about, not even as she clenched down a little more urgently around the vines filling her holes, her bondage restrictive, laid out there like a breeding dragon doll to be adored. They knew that she needed time, however, as much as Nessa wanted to be bred and impregnated all over again, laid into, right then and there, and she was forced to merely squirm and wriggle in their grasp, begging for what would only come in time.

Egg-laying, after all, was a pleasure delivered only by the breeding-plant and they would control their newest host body.

Nessa whimpered, tongue pushing out of her maw, dangling over between her teeth. It was all she'd ever wanted. But later would come the laying…

And that was something different entirely.

Tentacle Play

"Ohhhh…"

Verity moaned, the husky's head falling back as she quivered in the grip of the tentacles. Not many understood why she kept such a, supposedly, volatile plant in her back garden of all places but, well, the green and white husky most certain had her reasons for doing so. Even if others would not have understood.

Large, pink petals opened under her, though it was not an aggressive species in the slightest, not even with the tentacles twisting out from its centre in a soft shade of pastel green. Deciduous trees waved lightly in the wind above them, shading them in dappled sunshine from the last hour of the day. Soon, the leaves would turn orange and yellow and red in shades of Autumn, but, until then, Verity was protected and shaded, just as she wanted to be.

"Ah…" She panted heavily, her bare breasts rising and falling sharply, pink nipples showing through the white of her fur. "Good… Mmm… Oh, so good…"

She could barely get out any words at all, hoisted in the air as she was. Tentacles, or vines, technically, from the semi-sapient plant wound around her, holding her up comfortably, as if she was sitting back in a deep armchair. Her tail was left free to wag to her heart's content, however, flicking up in that traditional husky curl to show off her soft folds and the pucker of her tail hole.

It was a good thing, however, that Verity, always a green thumb in the garden, had grown tall trees at the border of her residential home – to block the view of the neighbours on days like that. The wind was up, which both muddied her cries and made them carry: a delicious conundrum to lock herself into.

The vines twisted around her thighs, a slender, green length tickling the pad of her foot-paw, though Verity trembled and resisted the urge to squeal. No, no… It would not do to cry out, not then, not when there was already so much going on. She could have the plants there, all manner of them, as long as they were not dangerous, but things would change very quickly if her neighbours got wind at all of what she was doing in her garden with those same plants.

The husky wasn't thinking straight, however, not as a curious tentacle pressed up to her pussy, the tip rounded and a little bulbous. She shivered. That one was one of her favourites: an egg-laying vine. She could not be fully impregnated by the plant, not able to carry anything that it deposited into her to term, but that didn't mean that the experience for the anthro canine was any less pleasurable.

"Mmmm… Oh, yes…"

The dog made everything quite clear as to what she wanted, the plant understanding her in some capacity. It knew what to do with a willing, squirming body like hers, however, teasing the vine over her pussy and clit, bringing the throbbing nub to a pulse of pleasure. Verity moaned – and the plant took advantage of that by stuffing a vine into her maw and up to the back of her throat. She could have gagged and choked but caught herself in time for the vine to squirt a numbing sap into her throat, so that she could take it down.

"Mmm…"

Her eyelids fluttered, her groan muffled. The canine didn't care, no, not in the slightest, not as another vine slipped into her pussy, smoothly prying open her folds to slide slickly through her arousal. Her pussy tried to squeeze around it reflexively, though it was only for the purposes of pleasure and not to stop it from getting inside her, increasing sensation as she trembled weakly.

It was the best place to be, the tentacle grinding back and forth, thickening up as it inflated inside her. It pumped up, straining at her pussy, sliding deeper, forcing her to stretch around it, even though Verity was very much on board with everything that was going on. The husky tried to buck her hips, raising her tail, though she couldn't stop wagging it, not as pleasure wracked her body.

It was thicker than any cock she had ever taken, the vines giving her everything that she could ever have wanted from a sexual partner, though the plant benefitted from using her body too. That was one of the reasons that they were so hard to keep in the country, with few wanting to indulge them, though it was no problem to Verity. No problem at all, not as she arched and ground back, doing all she could as she squirmed against the delicious restriction of the vines, letting them curl and coil and dig into her even more.

She ached for it, another pressing to the tight pucker of her tail hole as it squeezed inside, just applying a little pressure to let her know what she wanted. More and more slid into her body, the sensitive nerve endings at her pucker on fire, panting heavily through her nostrils as her maw was stuffed full.

"Mmph… Ohhhh…"

Verity tried to groan, so very needily, yet it was all coming along, her body prickling and tingling with fire, as if a tangible heat was creeping over her skin. If she grew hot enough, there was a wild part of the husky that feared it would sear the fur from her very skin, twisting back and forth, eyelids fluttering all the way closed as she succumbed completely to pleasure.

There was nothing else for it, not as she allowed the plant to use her, her pussy stuffed full, the double penetration on her bottom half simply divine. The dog thought she couldn't take anymore – and then the plant found a way to pump up its tentacles just a little more, swelling inside her and stimulating her as they lusciously ground back and forth, back and forth. It was not even about the slow, sinuous motion but how they dragged and pulled through her folds and her tail hole, her body aching with delight.

Orgasm, when it came, had no sense of time attached to it, rolling through her deliciously, her whole body shaking. She tried her best to grip the tentacles with her fingers, though there was only so much the husky could do when the vines were carefully kept away from her questing fingers, as much as she may have wanted to hold on to them. It would only have been a plaintive sense of stability that she got, however, for the vines were in control, the plant working its tentacles back and forth, grinding deep, taking all it needed from her.

She blinked, eyelids fluttering without opening her eyes, relishing in every sensation, even the pulse and twitch of her pussy clenching around the vine. Her backside was tight, so tight, there surely had to be no space left inside her, no, not at all... In a state of delirium, lusciously floating, she took it all, her stomach bloated and full as the tentacle, finally, slid tenderly by the barrier of her cervix to capture her womb.

"Mm..."

Grunting around the vine in her mouth, Verity tried to regain some frail form of control over herself, tonguing the tentacle, though all the husky managed to do was drool around it. The plant didn't mind that, making use of the additional lubrication and squashing the tentacle down against her tongue, trapping it between the lines of her teeth. It was not for the husky, after all, to tell the plant what she wanted when she wanted it: she just had to take it.

Another orgasm shook her, toes and fingers curling deliciously, trying to claw on to the moment, panting and heaving in harsh, dragging breaths. Yet Verity was right where she wanted to be, twisting and moaning, lifting her hips to the extent that she could, her tail twitching up another notch, just when the canine thought that she could not be more devious and exposure herself even more than before.

Her body always surprised her. The plant even more so.

The vine inside her pussy thickened up, bulge after bulge running down the length from the bud of the flower, where the tentacles emerged, to her pussy. She grunted and twitched, losing herself, not even able to track where one orgasm ended and the next began, riding the waves of pleasure as if there was to be no end, no end at all. Truthfully, Verity would have been more than happy to stay out there in the open, plundered by tentacles, letting her body be nothing more than a vessel for every egg that the plant deposited into her.

"Mmm… Nnngghhh…"

She could groan as loud as she wanted: no one would hear her. Not as she swayed and her pussy stretched viciously around the eggs within the vine, the tentacle laying them directly up into her womb. Of course, it secreted a lubrication that both allowed her body to relax around it and give her even more pleasure but without giving her any pain in the slightest. Despite the extreme that her body was being forced through, there was more still more to come.

Her belly bloated, inflating as the eggs jostled for space. They were large yet soft enough to bump up against one another with soft exteriors, not like the shells from bird eggs that she had been more familiar with before getting into plants: that had been a very different hobby, of course. Yet the stretch of her belly and womb straining to expand around them ached through her, forcing all else from her mind, though Verity doubted she could have thought about anything else at that time if she had even had the mental capacity for it.

No… That wasn't what her tentacle play was about, allowing the plant to lay egg after egg inside her, her belly swollen and lumpy, showing the definition of every egg that was shoved up against the front of her abdomen. She was there to experience every moment, to soak it all in, the tentacle in her ass thrusting more roughly, crudely taking her for the ride that she had so sorely needed. Yet it was all she ached for, whimpering and grunting, giving herself over entirely to nature as her body was wracked and rocked, over and over again.

The eggs bulged, yet there could only be so many of them as she tried her best to tongue the tentacle in her mouth, running her tongue around the tip when it drew back. The plant wasn't trying to make anything easier for her, not in the slightest, but she did appreciate the ability to breathe a little more easily through her mouth too, her muzzle lightly wrinkled as she twisted.

"Mmmph… Oh… Take me… Nnnghhh!"

And then the vine was back in her mouth, working roughly back and forth as every last egg pushed up into her womb. Her cervix tightened again, becoming harder and more unyielding, keeping them all inside. Later, when the time was right, she would lay them all out in the garden, unfertilised, and let them give the nutrients needed back to the garden, buried in the rich soil.

The plant would not know, but they still would lay more and more eggs inside her. And Verity would come back, each and every time, just for pleasure, for her own, kinky needs. That was fine, all of her own prerogative, though the husky would never reveal just how much she adored being plugged full of eggs, rolling through orgasm after orgasm, losing track of the time and place, just for her sordid ecstasy.

It was hers, all hers… Verity moaned, spinning in lust, the tentacles sliding back, thrusting, stimulating her to another, biting, sharp orgasm that had her hips bucking. According to research, it helped settled the eggs within a recipient's womb.

The husky didn't care. She just wanted to have her fun.

And the plant was the one that would always reap the spoils…

In the arms, of course, of a little tentacle play.

Their Tentacle Toy

Mina giggled and stretched out on the bed, the cow's hands back behind her head as her mare partner knelt between her legs, the pair naked already. The black and white cow had anthro features, with the breasts on her chest, though she still had a small, traditional pair of udders at the front of her crotch, which sometimes affected the clothes she was able to wear. However, Mina was more than comfortable with working with her body in that way, usually going for skirts rather than anything that pressed in tightly around her crotch and between her legs. It was all a matter of style for the bovine.

On the other hand, Cassie didn't have udders to speak of, just a pair of heavy breasts that perfectly complemented her voluptuous form. She was more heavily-built than Mina with wide hips and moderate shoulders, offering her a bottom-heavy hourglass figure. The cow had something more of a slenderer figure, though her breasts were larger rather than smaller, her hips broad enough to definitely be called feminine. But who was in charge, anyway, of deciding what was feminine and what was not? Mostly likely those who really should have had no say at all in it.

"So…" Mina chuckled, one of her large, black ears twitching lightly. "I hear you have a new toy for us to try…"

Cassie grinned and swished her tail, the palomino mare's hair falling in a sleek, glorious sheen.

"Yes!"

It was impossible for the equine to keep the glee out of her voice as she snatched the small, wooden "chest" from the bedside table, half-scrambling over the cow in her effort to be swift. The bedroom they shared was furnished in a modern style, though the pale pastels of blue and purple were not a style that everyone could have gone for. One wall was entirely taken up by wardrobes with mirrors on the exterior, so the room appeared lighter and airier with a fresh feel to it.

Of course, it was dim in the evening light with the lamps on the bedside table on a setting that cast a soft, warming glow over the bedroom, a handful of pink, slow-burning candles set on a shelf on the wall facing the bed to set the mood. Mina sat up on her knees before her partner as Mina curled her torso up, tightening her abs and feeling her body work to bring herself back to a sitting position.

"It's from the new sex shop," Cassie explained, though the mare's ears twitched back and forth, always reverting to focus on the cow, in her excitement. "I know you like the tentacle toy, the dildo... I thought something a little more real would be fun."

Mina eyed it suspiciously, though her lips pulled up in a curious smile, despite her mild trepidation.

"What...like one of the magic boxes with something kinky inside?" She asked, trying to get a better feel for what Cassie was offering. "Only...this time it'll be tentacles? For us?"

"Mhm!"

The mare nodded, blue eyes shining as she leaned forward, still clasping the box in both hands.

"It won't last more than a night, I think," she admitted with a soft splay to her ears and droop to her tail, "but that's something at least."

Mina's expression softened and she took the box from the horse, setting it gently aside on the bed.

"Cassie, hon... Those are expensive. They're one-time use."

"I know," Cassie murmured as the cow cupped her cheeks and traced her thumb across the right one. "But you're worth it, Mina. You're *always* worth it."

There was no other reply Mina could have had to that other than to kiss her partner, her tongue flitting right up against the mare's lips to coax them open. Not that Cassie would have denied her in any way, of course, but Mina wanted more than that, hungrily deepening the kiss as she led the way. Cassie moaned into the embrace, her hand fluttering up to the cow's breasts, thumbing across her nipple and drawing a low moo into the kiss itself.

She'd always been more on the adventurous side and having a touch of magic in their world at least meant there were more options still for pleasure. Sure, it could be a little on the pricey side for furs like them, but that wasn't really too much of a bad thing. Playing with some freaky little magical tentacles in a box was a far safer thing than wandering into the clutches of a tentacle monster out in the deep forest. As sensual as that could be too…

Cassie's fingers, however, twitched towards the box once more, as eager as ever to get started. She gently broke the kiss, though her blood was up and warm breath tickled her partner's lips and face as she heaved for it, nostrils fluttering and flaring. She was very glad indeed she was a mare and not a stallion for dealing with obvious arousal from just kissing her partner in public was not something she wanted to have to deal with in daily life either. Being a mare, she had the chance to keep things more discreet.

"Let's set it down here," she said with a lick of her lips, tasting Mina on them. "And then...we can just see what it does."

Mina nodded, the cow tilting her head slightly to the side as she studied the box.

"I guess we can keep the box afterwards to?"

Cassie snorted a laugh, eyeing her.

"Yes…" She said fondly, leaning forward to steal a swift, chaste kiss from the cow's lips. "You can have the box afterwards for your craft bits."

Mina smirked, tapping Cassie's nose.

"I'm going to crochet a tiny tentacle!"

"Of course you are."

Cassie shook her head, though she really would not have wanted her partner to be any other way than exactly who she was, as she was. The cow never failed to brighten her day and, where they sat and knelt, she put the box down between them on the bedsheets.

"I shouldn't have to do anything more than open it up," she murmured to herself. "So… Just one moment… There!"

She unfastened the box, which had a button and a clip that needed to be released with two hands (presumably so no one was assaulted by tentacles without their consent) and a soft, green glow emerged. Cassie inhaled deeply, feeling the magic of it sparkle through her senses, as if she had suddenly been rendered sharper and "zestier" than before. Her skin prickled all over and she couldn't help but lean forward expectantly, looking down into the box with her ears pricked to attention.

Mina was just as curious, though the cow spread her legs a little more and scooted some pillows forward on the bed so they could grab them while, well, otherwise incapacitated. They didn't have to wait for more than a few heart beats, however, before a slim, wriggling tendril appeared over the edge of the box, touching the exterior as if it was investigating its surroundings.

"Mmm…" Cassie breathed, eyes intent as more tentacles emerged from the box, some exploring their surroundings and others twisting in and out of their brethren, straight up from the box. "Oh, they're cute!"

"Are you going to still think they're cute when they're making you whinny in climax?"

"Probably."

But they didn't have a chance to keep chatting like that as the tentacles investigated, a deep, rich, forest green painting their "flesh." It was hard to say what the tentacles were actually made from, being magical, but they felt like the smoothest of skin as they brushed against Mina's inner calves and confidently crept up over her knees to her thighs. The tips were lightly rounded and tapered, but they were not much narrower than the length of the actual tentacles themselves. And they came in all manner of thicknesses, with some as thick around as Cassie's wrist, while Mina's wrists were a little smaller and more delicate than hers. Other tentacles were fine and questing, wriggling up along with the others as they set about exploring both of the ladies they were to enjoy that evening.

"Oooh... It kind of tickles..."

Cassie chuckled as the tentacle crept up her thighs where she knelt, winding its way around and around her leg, though she was not at all worried about it. Her tail swished wantonly back and forth and she grinned, licking her lips. Would one of them want to slide between her lips, wet and slick with a sheen of saliva like sweet, alluring lip gloss? Oh, she'd really like that, to taste them, to slide her fleshy tongue along a tentacle just to feel it pushing into the back of her mouth.

Mina grabbed her hand and they supported one another as the tentacles teased higher, reaching the tops of their thighs and caressing the very upper curve. The cow sucked in a breath as they brushed her folds, a tiny drop of moisture heralding her arousal, although Mina was more than willing to wait and see, to allow the magical toy to do its best to them both. If she interfered, who knew what she could be missing out on.

A slender tendril about the width of her finger teased along her plump folds, though did not quest higher to the cow's udders quite yet. Mina's breath hitched, a judder in her chest, as it brushed against her softness, before sweeping back down them to where her arousal marked her pussy lightly. It pushed inside as if that could be the only possible answer – and then withdrew, allowing a thicker tentacle to take its place.

The smaller one pushed her folds apart, Mina grunting, and swirled around her clit, twisting and curling back and forth, dragging over the increasingly sensitive nub of flesh. The cow moaned and tucked her chin down, clinging more tightly to her partner's hand, but she was there in the moment for her too and ready not to miss a single thing.

The mare, on the other hand, faced a tentacle grinding straight up to her tail hole, perhaps seeing it as the obvious option rather than her pussy. She squealed and rocked her hips, but was not at all averse to a little play there, lips parted as she grazed her partner's gaze with her own. Her tail lifted welcomingly and the tentacle pressed against her tight pucker, exuding a little of its own lubricant to ease the penetration for her.

"Ohhhh!"

She clung even more tightly to Mina, her free hand flying forward to rest on the cow's chest: perhaps a happy accident but one that had the bovine lightly rolling her eyes. It was anything for boobs when it came to that mare, honestly, but she didn't mind the attention. Instead, her eyes dropped to the tentacle shifting and thrusting as it powered boldly into the equine's rump while more still explored her pussy.

One slid between the mare's folds and Cassie squirmed, panting heavily as Mina's soft cries joined hers. She could almost imagine just how the cow felt, squeezing around the tentacle in her pussy as she was taken, though their fun with the tentacles was only just getting started. She rolled her hips forward, leaning back a little, and more tentacles crawled up over her ass as if to provide a seat for her, supporting her. There seemed to be far more tentacles coming from the box that was only about the size of both her hands together – but, then again, it was magic, so what more could Cassie really have expected there?

"Ah… Yes…"

The mare moaned as the tentacle separating the soft folds of her pussy eased back and found her sex, pushing inside with the slickness of her arousal to guide its way. She bucked her hips without thinking about what she was doing, trying to sink on to both tentacles at once as another, smaller one opened up to "suck" on her clit.

Her cry echoed through the room and Mina swore the candle flames danced, but it wasn't something she could bring up in a moment like that, no, not as the tentacles playing with her pussy and clit sent rippling waves of pleasure coursing through her. She loved a slow build-up and, somehow, the magical tentacles knew that too, gently working her over as her juices flowed freely and she squeezed luxuriously around the thick intrusion filling her cunny.

"Mmm, I can't wait to see you orgasm," Mina breathed, her gaze locked with Cassie's refusing to release her partner as the curvy mare whimpered and, to get her own back, groped the cow's breast. "You're going to be even more beautiful than always, head thrown back, trying to hurl yourself down to the bed… I think even more tentacles will take you then, squirming all over you, squeezing your tits, another filling your mouth."

"Ohhhh, you tease me so…"

Cassie moaned, but she was right where she needed to be, enjoying the delicious throb of being penetrated in her ass and pussy at once. The two tentacles teased up against one another through the thin barrier of flesh that separated them and she couldn't help but wriggle in place, wanting to demand more and yet not quite knowing how to do that. How did a mare "demand" anything of a magical object?

Maybe I should have done more research into this…

It was too late for that, though only good things lay ahead for the two femfurs, holding on to one another as they rocked their hips and moaned. Mina leaned back, wanting to pull the mare along with her, but Cassie only tipped forward increasingly, her tail lifted as the tentacles worked in tandem to stuff her full. A lewd, wet squelch rose from her pussy as she was fucked – it was crude, but, really, there was simply no other word for it – and the mare nickered, eyes half-closed in passion.

So, Mina did not sit back all the way but grabbed one of the pillows she'd edged down, pushing it under her buttocks right at the back to raise them slightly. It gave the cow a little more to bounce on as the tentacle ground into her, though the other tentacles had not been idle in the slightest.

They slithered up her body like winding, twisting snakes, finding her breasts and wrapping luxuriously around them. Mina sucked in a breath, watching her breasts rise – and then grunted in the back of her throat as the tentacles caught her by surprise, playing over her udders too. They slid between the teats and curled over the top, gently squeezing and testing out what made her moan, the cow's body sensitive to such a touch.

Her breasts were encircled by two, almost loving, tentacles that only had pleasure in mind for her, while the rippling twists of arousal rolling out from her clit dug deeper still into her body. Such pleasure, after all, was never meant to be set aside under any circumstance and she leaned hungrily into it, trembling where she sat with her legs spread in a wide V-shape.

Cassie, however, was not as willing to hold back as the cow was, holding on tightly to her as her head bowed and a curious tentacle probed at her lips. Shivering with delight, sweat gently darkening her hide, she parted her lips with interest for it, lapping over the head and sliding it around the tip. It welcomed the entrance into her mouth and ground over her tongue as she slurped, eyes fluttering closed. With so much sensation to lean into, even the bedsheets creasing under her knees, she wanted to sink even more into it all, not missing a single thing.

The tentacle pushed right up into the back of her throat as if it had no care at all for going slowly and gently – which was exactly how Cassie wanted it to act. She wanted to be taken hard and rough, now that she was warmed up, pursing her lips around the tentacle so she could suck as hard as possible. The ones in her pussy and ass sped up, near enough making her head spin, though she still fluttered her eyelids apart to steal a look at her partner, the love of her life with whom she was sharing the moment.

The cow was spectacular, her cloven hooves kicked out wide as her pussy was plundered. Every time the tentacle drew back slightly, it gleamed with a sheen of her arousal and Cassie whimpered, wanting to lap the tentacle clean, not wasting a single drop. She'd have more than enough time, after the magic was done, to eat out her partner with raw, vivacious passion, but that was not for that moment. She had to ease into it, to learn how to relish in every thrust and every shudder of arousal, her body tightening around both tentacles as she squeezed. What was ever the point of sex if not to revel in every single moment, after all?

She groaned, however, as two more tentacles made their way up to her breasts. They did not wind around her boobs as they did for the cow, however, and the mare panted heavily through her nostrils as they opened up to latch on to her nipples. A pleasant suction rolled through her chest, as if they were trying to milk her, or pull her nipples out and away from her chest, leaving her squirming and heaving for breath more than ever.

It was much too much, the cord of tension in her body drawing tauter as the tentacles pleasured her, although Cassie was more than willing to go there. Oh, she was very much willing, enjoying the others that held on to her thighs, steadying her, and crawled over her ass, teasing up even under the velvety dock of her tail and the exceedingly soft skin that was to be found there. She moaned around the tentacle in her mouth, her saliva coating it, trying to lock her eyes on the cow and finding all she had was a squeeze of her boob and, of course, her hand too. The tentacle arched, blocking too much of her vision, the mare having no option left other than to submit to it.

Mina, however, was more in control of her body, even as her heart beat raced and blood roared in her ears. Desire surged through her, a force no one was ever meant to restrain when it was so beautifully received, and she rocked her hips, leaning into the tentacles that wound around her waist and lower back, trusting them to support her. The tentacle in her pussy thrust all the way up to her innermost barrier, though never slammed into it, always knowing exactly how deep it could go.

She grunted, licking her lips, though the mare's muffled cries were more than enough to get her going, her tail trying to flick back and forth, although Mina was partway sitting on it. The cow panted heavily, parting her lips but still inhaling sharply through her nostrils, yet there was nothing she could do to ease the tension in her body other than give in to the high of orgasm – when it came, that was.

Mina wriggled her hips, rocking her weight first into one and then the other, heat pouring through her. Her pussy squeezed erratically around the tentacle, only hindering it ever so slightly from thrusting, but she still smirked inwardly at making its job there ever so slightly more difficult. She didn't want to harry it, of course, but she still wanted to feel every slick inch grinding into her, her eyes flicking to her deliriously moaning partner, the mare quivering as if she was right on the edge of orgasm already.

Oh, she'll definitely be the first to go.

But Mina was more than happy with that, licking her lips wetly and huffing a panting breath as she fixed her gaze on Cassie. The palomino mare with the golden-hued coat was spellbinding and, even then, she would have been hard-pressed to take her eyes off her, wanting to be there for every, single throbbing moment.

Cassie cried out, her whole body juddering for a second, the crush of orgasm upon her. Her pussy rippled around the tentacle and her ass clenched, but there was no rhythm to the tight squeezes, only her body releasing everything it needed to. A heady rush of her arousal painted the tentacle slamming ruthlessly into her sex with a slick sheen, the friction exquisite as her head spun and spun.

She was lost there, aware of Mina's boob under her hand and the cow's hand clutching hers, but little more than that swam through the pleasure. She moaned lewdly, caught in the moment, her body aching through wracking ecstasy that stripped her down to nothing at all and then back up again. The tentacle burst from her mouth in a light splatter of drool, a moan rolling from her lips, and she tried to follow it, the pink of her tongue extended as if to capture it for her own once more.

It danced away, however, as the tentacles "sucked" on her nipples, drawing out her orgasm more and more. Electric sparks of pleasure darted through her as she was stimulated in more ways, a broader tentacle grinding over her pussy too as it caught her aching, lightly throbbing clit. She would have said she was too sensitive as her high drew her on, panting loudly, but the mare knew well enough that she could have gone again already.

She was ready for anything the night threw at her – and everything the tentacle box had to offer.

Mina got to see every expression crossing her partner's face, lips parted in sensual bliss, her body warmed and primed. The tentacles relaxed their grip on the mare, allowing her to recover, but that only meant they doubled down on their "attack" of Mina.

And she had no intention of holding back, licking her lips, hungry for her girlfriend as the mare recovered, her white mane spilling so sweetly over her face that the cow wanted to brush it back, tenderly framing her face once more. The cow groaned long and low, so deep it almost sounded like a moo, her body tensing increasingly as climax called to her.

The tentacles squeezed around her breasts, but it was the one curling around her clit, joined by a second, that brought her over the edge. The stimulation was simply too sweet with the slow, persistent thrusting into her sex, stretching her open perfectly. Her nostrils flared, striving to drag in breath, yet she let out a bellowing groan all the same, as loud in the moment as she had ever been. If she'd been wholly in her right mind, she would have caught the flash of a grin across Cassie's face for her being louder, though it was all in good fun for the two of them.

As long as they were together, nothing could ever be wrong.

Mina's hips thrust lightly, getting the most out of the moment as the tentacles did their work and her body flooded with pleasure, ecstasy spiking out from her clit, her sex soaked with arousal. She didn't care for how wet she was, even as the tentacle moved more swiftly with the added wetness, but she was ready for it, clinging to Cassie's hand and steadying herself through it. As the tentacle's lust swept through her, she relished in it all, determined to enjoy every last little second to the fullest, even as her warming bliss, slowly, tapered off.

When she came back to her senses fully, she caught the mare's eye, the tentacles still, gently, thrusting within their chosen holes. Another tentacle probed around to Mina's glutes, as if it was trying to find her tail hole too, although she squirmed, unsure yet as to whether or not to allow it entry.

Maybe she would, maybe she wouldn't… She winked at Cassie, who nickered with a certain kind of gleam in her eye. Whatever she chose, it would be for her pleasure – and Cassie's too, of course.

"Another round?" Cassie offered, squeezing her hand. "We could slip into a more comfortable position. And it's not as if the tentacles are done yet."

Mina grinned.

"Absolutely… And, this time, I'm getting off first!"

"Only if I don't!"

Together, laughing, they collapsed back on the bed with the tentacles coming with them, the femfurs in one another's arms and their lips on each other's. There was no better place to be as the tentacles pleased them, ecstasy bringing them to orgasm after orgasm that night.

Their tentacle toy might well turn out to be their favourite toy of all…

Tentacle Dreams

Miguel groaned, the young man standing tall and firm on the edge of the cliff. Dressed only in a pair of shorts and a loose T-shirt with a faded band name on the front, he did not appear like a man who was out hiking on one of the Greek islands. After hopping from one to the other for the last couple of weeks, Miguel had lost track of where he had been and where he was, his light brown skin darker than it usually was, though it took a lot for him to tan, considering the natural colour of his skin. His hair lay around his ears in dark, black curls, shining ever so slightly with the dampness of sweat, though his lips were parted in anticipation of what to come.

"Where are you?"

He stared out before him, the whisper on his lips, tipping forward. The cliff dropped down sharply to the ocean, the stone and hard-packed dirt that made it up jagged and cut as if it had been shaped by a giant's hand. It was far beyond Miguel, but he was there to face his fears, to take on the challenges in life that he had turned away from so far, even though he wanted to face them.

To an outside observer, he could very well have been on the precipice of doing something ridiculous, something so very dangerous that it would be hard to believe and even harder to prevent. But Miguel knew what he was doing, as crazy as it looked.

He took a deep breath, his narrower chest expanding, ribs lightly pulling through the skin that covered his ribcage. His light, lithe body had trained for years for such an act. And he was not the most well-known free jumper for nothing.

This jump, however, boasted a prize unlike any other at the bottom.

He spread his arms, bending his knees, relishing in the moment before his leap of faith, before he threw all manner of caution to the wind, playing with death and taunting it with his smile. The seagulls called, whipping and wheeling, and other ocean birds that he did not know the names of, but wherever he went, there were always gulls to be had. They were the one bird that stretched to every corner of the globe and their calls soothed him, the frantic beating of his heart coming off the pace just a jot. He had to be calm if he was going to jump.

Miguel did not remember the exact moment of hurling his body into freefall, only the sensation of the wind rushing by him, not a cry on his lips but his lips parted sensually all the same. He sent his praises up to any listening gods as he plunged down, the deep blue water calling him, tipped with foam, his life complete as he showed off just what being a free jumper was all about. Leaping from cliffs and taking his life in his hands – it was what his life was all about, what he yearned for, what gave him life. Yet he needed the prize of what lurked secretly beneath the surface of the water even then.

He never touched down in the water – not under his own volition, that was. A tentacle wound in purple and green, plant-like, threads whipped out and snapped around him, slimier than he could have expected as it twined around his body. Miguel's cry was cut short and he had only a moment to hold his breath as the tentacle rushed back beneath the surface of the water, plunging deeper and deeper, churning up the water in the wake of it. It frothed and writhed and there was no stopping it as he was yanked under the water, the sparkling surface darting far away from him as if it was the water that was racing away from him and not him moving through the water.

His heart surged, chest tight with breath that he needed to take. Yet he was right where he wanted to be, crying out his longing for the water, the tentacle that had taken him, though it was sure that no one else would have had the same reaction as him. Maybe he was wrong: maybe it was a thrill that more sought. Maybe it was just him though that lusted for the embrace of a tentacle that he thought that, perhaps, only he understood and no one else ever could. He'd been there once before, after all.

The tentacle twisted deeper, snaking into an underwater cavern and hurling him up – up and up and *up*. There seemed to be no end to it but not even Miguel could tell anymore which way was up as his clothes floated around him, embraced by the water and desperately trying to relieve themselves of his body even then.

And then air – fresh air! He dragged in a lungful, not even caring how it was possible, water streaming from his face, hair sodden and clinging.

He gasped for breath, tossed up into a cave that seemed to hold a pocket of air underwater, the walls streaming with seawater, the trickle and drip of it impossible to escape. Yet Miguel was not given anything more than a moment to collect himself as the tentacle slithered around him again, slick and smooth and inherently plant-like. It was not a creature that lived and breathed but it was of the world in which he lived, something that rooted itself amongst kelp and reproduced with those like Miguel who wanted to invade its territory. Maybe not all that had come into the tentacle monster's domain had been willing, but the gasp and moan on Miguel's lips conveyed his willingness openly and vocally.

"Oh... Yes..." He groaned, twisting his head back and forth as the vine-like tentacle squirmed up his shorts, ripping them from his skin, his T-shirt following a moment later. "Yes... Please... Oh, fuck..."

It was every one of his wildest fantasies come true as more and more tentacles shot from the water, dripping with moisture, splattering him with seawater. They took him for their own, winding around and wrapping him up, hefting him bodily from the rough, stone floor as if he weighed nothing at all. Yet he was a lighter sort of man, his cock rising to full mast, as he arched and tried to show his willingness, lips parted but caught up in so many breathy moans that just getting out what he wanted in a moment like that was simply beyond him.

It was all for him though as the tentacles – so many twisting around and around – adored him. They were gentle with him, well, as gentle as tentacles could be. But Miguel could not have honestly said that he wanted them to be gentle, no: not when they could be crude, pounding and grinding, questing tips wriggling up against the suddenly exposed pucker of his anal ring. He could have clenched down, shaken his head, tried to force it back out, but that was not what he needed to do, not even then, letting out a throaty moan as he rolled his hips back eagerly into the tentacles' questing, curious thrusts.

"Y-yes…"

He wasn't sure if he managed to get the word out, but he had a muffled moan for the tentacles as one rammed its way into his mouth, pressing down over his tongue without pushing into the back of his throat. He was glad of that – that would have been too much for his gag reflex straight away, something he could not have taken immediately. He needed time, just to be warmed up, moaning around it, another tentacle suitably slimed-up and penetrating his backdoor entrance. That commanded his attention even as he tried to suck in a breath through his nostrils, the curves of them flared as if they were nowhere near enough to drag in all that he needed.

However, it was hard to worry about or even think of anything at all like that while his pucker tried to close down around the tentacle. He had to force himself to relax, to allow it deep, even as another sucked his shaft into a tiny opening that was like a mouth but stretched perfectly to fit his hard length. Miguel twisted his head back and forth, arching his back and bucking in such delirious pleasure that it was a struggle even to contain it, panting around the tentacle in his mouth and yet still sucking on it as if it was a cock. He'd done a fair share of that in his life but there was nothing and no one quite like the tentacle monster to take him to the height of tentacle dreams and passions.

The tentacles, however, had their own needs to be met and one man suckling sweetly on an appendage was not going to do it for them. Turning him upside-down to suit their whims, they pounded him full, allowing their secretions to soften and loosen him up even more, pushing into his throat as his gag reflex too was numbed. Miguel moaned and half-closed his eyes but the driving pound of it all was something that would come and come whether his body was ready for it or not.

More... The hazy thought rose through a clamour of lust, cock hard and desperate to cum. He had to have more, so much more, twisting his head but not really moving at all, the tentacles luxuriously controlling all that he had to give them. They would take it from him still and he leaned heavily into their control, wanting to give it all up to them as his skin crawled with the sensation of the tentacles writhing and wrapping and his heart pounded viciously. There was nothing gentle to be had with a tentacle monster, after all, the plant that had dragged him down, once again, to its lair in the depths, and he wouldn't have been there if softness and sweetness was anything of what he had wanted to begin with.

No... No. It was better to moan, to feel a tentacle slide down his throat, taking over his breathing for him, though he still could not have explained how it did that. Miguel did not care as it oozed something slick and enticing down his throat, his body leaping for it, craving it even though he had never actively tasted it. His backdoor entrance was sore but in a good way, though he could not even rock back on to the tentacle's thrusts, a man trapped and controlled by them in the only way that he could have ever imagined. Stretched so far, it should have been impossible, a second tentacle writhing its way up into his anal passage, forcing him to submit to them.

Yet could he ever be forced when he would have thrown himself on his knees, again and again, for the tentacle monster and its wrath? Oh, Miguel's blood sang for the passion of them, how his cock was suckled, pulsed and massaged, better than any human mouth could have been. The tentacle monster's strokes sped up, pounding his ass in rampant, alternating strokes, never leaving him empty but getting more from him than before, his lips pressing down around the snake of a tentacle in his mouth, betraying a needy whimper.

There was no holding off, a broken, muffled howl bursting from his lips, cum pouring from his cock. There should have been spurts, but that was not to be so as he was milked for all he was worth, the tentacles taking everything from him, even what he had not thought his nuts were there to give. His seed was drawn from him expertly and his head swam, pulsating waves of ecstasy coursing through, even though he could not even buck and thrust his hips. It was a luxury, in a way, to have that liberty taken from him, his body simply that of a broken soul who longed to hit that next high, to get to that next peak of pleasure.

The tentacles narrowed his world. There was nothing more for him as his pucker tightened further around the fat appendages – or had they simply shoved another one entirely into him? There was no way to tell with his head spinning in such a way, ecstasy overcoming him, his body turned first one way and then the other as his body was made good use of. The tentacles seemed to enjoy him, thrusting madly, wildly, an untamed creature that he could not put a name to. They were everything they had been before and hungrier too, pushing on, squeezing just a little deeper as if, even then, they were testing his limits.

They had more, however, more than he had not even anticipated. For his first visit was not the penultimate one as they rumbled and churned within him, the tentacles trembling as if something greater was coming. Miguel's brow furrowed but all was to be revealed as he squinted, a lump travelling down the tentacle rammed into his mouth. There was no escaping it so all he could do was moan as he welcomed it in, his lips parted as wide as his jaw would allow to take it deep, to allow it down. One lump followed another, however, as he was filled, the lumps pouring down into his stomach where something round and soft jostled up against another round and soft thing in the pit of his stomach.

Eggs... He thought dimly. They were eggs. It was a plant but it was still, somehow, managing to lay eggs in him.

And he was proud to use his body as a vessel for the tentacle monster, moaning as more and more cum was milked from his cock, his shaft over-sensitive but still forced to give all that it could. There was no longer any pleasure to his ongoing orgasm, milked and used, but there was a surge in his head that made up for it, dropping into an even more submissive frame of mind as his moans were swallowed up by the tentacles.

His pucker strained, taking egg after egg, though the secretions of the tentacles and the softness of the eggs, which could not have had any kind of hard shells, helped a little. Still, they had to find a seat in his stomach, worming and wriggling and forced up through his guts, his body accommodating them as the tentacle monster had known he would. Maybe it was why he had been drawn back there again after his first experience, craving the pleasure and luxury of it all, his body swelling, stomach plumping out and out and out.

For his body had to make room for every last one of those eggs as they filled his belly, jostling for space, pushing against one another as the tentacles caressed his rising stomach. His abdomen bloated and he would have run his hands over it if he had been free to do so, though the tentacles were more than happy to do that for him, giving him and his body all that it desired. The sensitivity of touch softened in comparison to the ruthless pounding, his stomach inflated to the point that it looked as if he was at least six months pregnant and still growing. Yet that contrast had to be had to sweeten the deal as thick secretions filled the space around the eggs, ensuring that his body would be a soft, cushioning vessel for them and easing the outlines of the eggs that showed through the skin of his stomach.

More and more filled him, inflating him, using his body. And it was all that Miguel wanted as he was turned and rolled in the loving arms of the tentacles, his body where it, finally, needed to be. No more was he just a man but he was a man who had a use, his body swollen so much that his belly was growing larger than even the rest of him, a dominating feature that would, of course, make it difficult to move. Not that he would need to move at all while he was incubating the eggs, the tentacles feeding his own cum back through to fertilise them, though the uses that his body had for the tentacle monster were things still yet to come to light.

Until then, all he needed to be was to be a good host, not needing to move, rolled and cradled there, his grossly distended stomach supported by the tentacles. They wrapped around him and set him in a position that could have been sitting, his legs bent a little with his stomach spilling over them. One would have been hard-pressed to see the man behind his stomach, but he shakily brought his hands to his belly as the tentacles released him just a little, that tiny flexibility of movement all that he needed to satisfy himself, to moan luxuriously, a tentacle still in his mouth.

That tentacle would be needed to keep him fed and breathing, of course, but only time would tell for how long he would need to keep the eggs inside him, his stomach twice the size of his body and spilling to the sides, not a perfectly smooth round. The secretions that filled in around the eggs helped a little but also weighed him down even further, which could not be helped. The tentacles would make sure that he got all that he needed though as the last vestiges of cum were drawn from him and planted right where they belonged in the mass of the tentacle monster's eggs.

Only time would see just how the eggs would grow, but Miguel was not thinking about any of that, warm and comfortable, his skin dry but still a little slick with the natural secretion of the tentacle monster. He was where he needed to be and there was no more concern about it to be had than that, letting drowsiness take over, so full and so comfortable that it was impossible not to drift off.

Away and down... He sank. The eggs jostled within him, but they were there to rest, no harm to come to them. He would wake again to be pounded, the tentacles carefully repositioning the eggs inside him so that all may benefit, that all may be comfortable, yet, until then, it was time to rest.

Who knew that sweet tentacle dreams could come from such fervent meetings?

His Special Plant

Drew hummed a tune to himself, the small dragon collecting his gardening supplies before heading out into his back garden. He was lucky he lived in a more private area, with the neighbours set apart a little from one another, although he didn't have the same interests as others in his immediate neighbourhood. Transforming the glorious wilderness of flowers and bushes in his garden into something sculpted and manicured, "suitable for presentation" to the wider community, would have been a travesty to him.

The dragon's green scales were well polished, though they gleamed with such a sheen to them that they had the appearance of an oil stain, with blues and richer greens still twisting through the hue of a single colour. In different lights, his scales could look different – which was something of an issue when it came to things such as passports and identification. Drew's horns, at least, were small and elegantly curved with a slight rise to them that brought them out a little from the sides of his head. The points tapered, but he filed them carefully so they would not be as sharp: there was no need for that.

A feathery, soft mane ran down his back, starting at the point between his horns and following the line of his spine all the way down to the tip of his tail where it cumulated in a brilliant plume. The teal of the fluffy mane practically glowed and he took great pride in a plethora of products he used to keep it as fine and as silky as it was. Drew was only grateful in that regard that he didn't have fur all over his body like some dragons – and, of course, many mammalian anthros too. It seemed like a dreadful bother to keep clean and to dry after showering.

His tail was short enough that it was no trouble at all for Drew to keep it lifted from the ground, though his head only came up to about the height of a door handle in a standard, anthro home. Of course, Drew walked was a quadruped rather than a biped, but there were quads like him living in normal society too – if society could ever be considered normal. It was a way of living, admittedly, that made things a little difficult, considering how everything was designed for anthros of a certain height, more or less.

He managed well enough, at least. He could stand on two legs to use his little kitchen and was comfortable enough balancing like that as long as he had his tail to help steady him or even letting his front feet rest on a counter, maybe chopping vegetables, but he preferred the parts of his home – and the garden too – that were better adapted for a dragon of his size.

He didn't draw too much attention out in his neighbourhood or work, going to his office job and back again: it was nothing special to Drew and working on spreadsheets was most certainly not what got him out of bed in the morning. No, the dragon was most at home in the natural world or simply working on his garden, trotting between the beds of wildflowers and critically eyeing the weeds for ones to pull and ones to keep.

Some were cloying, twisting into the plants that offered food to bees and butterflies, required in the ebb and flow of the natural world. Dandelions were one such plant and his friends had once teased him for carefully replanting dandelions when he had cultivated his garden a little more carefully to sprays of colour and plants that complemented one another. He liked to remove some weeds, where they were crowding out other plants, but there was so much that needed care and weeds too had their purpose. Dandelions, after all, provided some of the first food for insects after the chill of winter. So, it was wrong to remove them entirely and, if he cut any for his teas, he made sure to leave the head of the plant behind, watching the leaves re-grow with pleasure. Their resilience was astounding.

He padded lightly out into the garden that afternoon, having taken some time off work, with another goal in mind, the dragon ducking his head as he passed through the section of the garden where the hedge bordering his property was lower. It was not that he didn't want to talk to Steve that day, the fox who lived close liking to wave over to him from his deck over in his garden, but he had business to attend to.

Well, not business...but it felt important. After all, Drew had purchased a very special new plant that needed a kind of care only he could provide. He wouldn't feel comfortable leaving the plant in the care of someone else if he had to go away until he had established a routine with it, but he was sure that was something he could overcome in time.

So, he had to start then, carrying a pail of tools in his mouth as he broke into a light trot, claws trimmed short enough not to cut into the grass and loam beneath. His new plant had been called a Hydras, though it seemed something of a colloquial name, named for the multiple tentacle-like vines it boasted, that it was able to twist and curl of its own accord. There were eight on a healthy plant, but his, so far, only had seven. He was determined to help it grow that eighth, checking the pH of the soil daily and adjusting the nutrients fed to it whenever instinct told him it was necessary.

"Hello, my beauty."

He murmured almost shyly as he approached the plant that was, at that time, smaller than he was. The bud was closed up tightly with the petals all furled together, as if no one would ever be able to hook fingers or claws into them in an attempt to open it up to the world. The soft petals had a purple hue to them, shifting through several shades until they reached violet, paler than he'd ever seen it before, at the tip of the bud, where they all closed in together. At the base of the plant was four large leaves, all splayed out to capture as much sunlight as possible, the seven vines lightly curling and twisting in the grass around it.

Drew had set the plant, allowing it to sink its roots down into the ground, in a shady spot of his garden with taller pine trees, near the end of his property, overshadowing it. That was what the salesfur had told him to do and his research only had corroborated the information he'd been given, though it seemed strange to have it hidden away like that. It was a rather private part of his garden too, feeling secluded and peaceful, so maybe it was the right place for it, after all.

He set the pail down and gently stepped around the plant, poking at the soil with his nose. Drew flicked out his tongue to taste the soil, though he was not quite as skilled in filtering through the different minerals and such that his taste buds could discern as he would have liked. Hopefully, that skill would grow in time.

"Oh!"

He twitched as a vine poked at his tail, sliding against the scales and then retreating from the fluff as if it had been surprised by a different texture. Drew chuckled and shook his head, letting his tail curl against the vine with the smooth, rounded tip, which was more defined than the rest of the placid, almost innocent length. It was almost like there was a "head" to the tentacle, almost seed shaped, but the salesfur had not given him much information about that. In fact, when he'd asked about the plant's care, wanting to pick their brain, they'd seemed very anxious and stuttered, fleeing with a stumble as if they'd wanted to be anywhere else than with a customer.

They probably had a lot of work to do that day, the dragon reasoned, though his mind wasn't really on that. *The vines are really curious today though…*

They had not been as active in the week he'd had the plant, letting it acclimatise to the new soil and care before he treated the vines to the "massage" he'd been told they needed. That was going to be a tricky part of the plant's care, he was sure, but the dragon was confident he'd be able to make it all work with his claws. He just had to be gentle and to take his time. It was not the reason he'd taken the afternoon off from work, to be fair, but knowing there was nothing else exerting pressing needs on his time relaxed him further: the perfect state in which to do the work.

"Can you come here?" He said softly to the plant, though Drew squirmed and tucked his tail down. "Wow, I feel silly…"

Was the plant a sentient being? Could it be? No, no… It was just a plant, even if its vines instinctively moved around it, seeking its own surroundings. It seemed there was much more for him to learn about the plant as he had been focused, first and foremost, on its care rather than researching more deeply into its origins and just what its effect on the world around it was. It was large enough that he'd thought it might need to be fed insects or other sustenance like some of the carnivorous varieties, but it apparently needed none of that, which was strange.

Still, he didn't enjoy feeding even passed creatures to carnivorous plants (that was why he kept the varieties that mostly trapped their own food, and those were few), so he was grateful not to have to consider that. Again, he tried speaking to the plant, keeping his tone low and soothing, as lacking in threat as he thought it possible.

"Hey, I'm just here to look after you," he said, running the smooth curve of the back of a claw over the nearest vine, which twitched under his touch. "There's nothing to worry about, but I do so wish you'd tell me everything you needed. I just want to give you all the best. How about a little vine massage?"

Two more vines joined the one playing over his claws and tapped around his front feet, one sliding under his body. The dragon stayed still, swallowing hard. He still didn't know how tough the vines were, if they would stand up to an accidental step or a cut from his shorter claws, and didn't want to risk it yet. It would be too sad if he lost the plant so soon after getting it – and, truth be told, Drew was rather attached to it already.

"Hey, little thing," he murmured, a smile tugging at his lips as the vines crawled curiously around his front legs, twisting up and around his lower limbs. "You're a curious little thing, aren't you? Nice and active…"

His research had told him the plant should be active and would likely crawl over him, sometimes twisting around his body, so that was not too much of a concern to him. One vine rose before his face and he stepped in a little closer, exceedingly careful not to stand on the vines laying in the grass, though there seemed to be more of them than ever. The plant seemed to be exuding a greater scent, something light flowing over his muzzle, practically begging him to inhale deeply and take in all he could.

"Mmmm…"

Drew hummed his appreciation and swung his tail lightly – and then found he couldn't, not as a vine curled around it. He shivered, the scales of his cheeks and neck warming, as his tail was held as if by a lover. But a plant was not to know that was a very intimate touch to be had between dragons, clasping tails in that manner. He tried to tell himself the plant was just exploring him, though, as he tugged and inhaled that scent, richly floral with an odd hint of spice laced through, but it felt like more than that.

It felt...*intimate.* Could that be right?

"Okay, so I'll just massage you here..."

The plant slithered off his right foot as he turned his paw so the claws faced up, gently holding up a vine so that it ran between his claws and over the sole of his foot. It tickled faintly and he couldn't help a giggle from jumping to his lips. The plant seemed to like it, however, shivering in his hold as he tested what kind of pressure he could apply to make it happy. There should really be no concern to massaging it, not like that, yet he licked his lips and enjoyed the moment, laying the vine back down so he could knead over it with the backs of his claws.

However, the plant was far from idle and he shivered in turn, leaning into it a little more, as the vines twisted around his hind legs, wrapping their way up his limbs like snakes. Yet it felt good, like he was being rooted in place, safe and secure. It was not a feeling Drew had enjoyed before and he wanted more of it, despite how his scales warmed all over, tingling.

"Let me..."

He breathed as he caressed one of the vines, letting it bop against his muzzle, though the dragon would not have been wrong in the slightest to suggest the plant was becoming more sensual with every passing moment. Drew had expected to be cool in the shade and yet a rise of heat flushed through his scales with every brush of the vines against him, still inhaling the beautiful aroma. It had become so much more than him merely enjoying and caring for his garden, although the drake was not at all against how the plant wanted him near.

Oh…

He swallowed hard as the vine twisted up and under his tail, caressing the sensitive scales there that were not touched all that often. It was not a place he had anticipated going, but the vine seemed to "accidentally" drag over his tail hole, stimulating the nerve endings clustered there.

"Ah, maybe not there? Let me…"

Yet the plant could not understand him and, at the end of the day, it was just a plant and wanted what it wanted. It sought heat and light and sustenance in the soil. And there was a little something more that the salesfur had not quite been willing to impart to Drew, his research not filling him in on how to make the plant flourish in his garden. He would have come to it in time, however, and the outcome would have been all the same, but a truly resourceful Hydras knew how to care for itself too.

Drew's tongue flickered out against his lips and the right side of his muzzle as he squirmed, finding the vines holding him firmly in place – but that was not a bad thing. The drake rocked back into them as the vines pulled his tail up a little higher, yet it was a nice feeling when they supported the weight of it as nicely as they did. It was as if the vines were trying to make his experience of the moment easier for him, taking the heaviness from his body.

Blushing hard, though the heat did not show through the dragon's scales, Drew let the plant explore him, even as its touch swept between his hind legs, reaching more erogenous zones. He didn't know if it was meant to happen, but it was too easy to go along with it, the botanist in him curious as to whether the plant was trying to stimulate him directly. It could not do any harm, even if he had never allowed his member out from its protective slit in the garden before.

No… If Drew had felt the "need" rise in him while he'd been out gardening, the drake had been quick enough to scurry back inside to take care of himself. His anatomy was quite humble for a dragon as his tail hole was tucked under the root of his tail and closed up quite tightly, so it was imperceptible to the majority of eyes. His actual genitalia was hidden within his lower abdomen, a slit allowing only his rather thick shaft out when needed, but his testes were always kept within his body. It was a feature some dragons had and Drew had always been glad for the modest notes of his body, for how it allowed him to roam in society more easily. Dragonesses could get away with wearing long dresses or other fashion items (styles changed), but drakes tended to go bare-scaled, unless they had a reason to hide something for the purposes of modesty.

He didn't want to hint to everyone how big his cock was, though the plant played two vines with those thicker "heads" around the slit under his belly, as if it knew exactly what to do. Squirming, he rocked his weight from one hind foot to the other, pushing back with his front feet.

"Ah…"

He let out a soft cry, forgetting entirely about the massage he'd promised to the Hydras' vines – for it seemed the plant had found something else to amuse itself with and he didn't trust himself to move anyway. His slit parted gently and the vines wriggled as if in excitement, almost seeming like they wanted to squirm their way into his slit. Yet Drew didn't know how much thought he was applying to the plan and its intent; he could only let things progress with heat prickling down his neck and his tail twisted up over his back.

Something slick dripped on to the tight ring of his tail hole and he wriggled, wondering at it. It felt went and like it wanted to run down, so it wasn't too viscous, though the plant's vine bore against it as he half-closed his eyes, rounding his back as need flared with him. His shaft protruded from his slit as the vines rubbed and curled against it, coaxing out the smooth, thick length, and the dragon let out a light, mewling cry.

He didn't want to be too loud, however – for what would he do if his neighbours, even if they were further away, heard him making sounds like that? He was sure they wouldn't be able to see him with the trees towering above him, offering him a welcome kind of shade, but they might well come to investigate if he shouted in any way.

No… He had to be soft, even though the moans didn't quite feel like they should have been rising from his throat as readily as they were. The dragon rocked his weight from one hip to the other and leaned back, the vine under his tail pushing against his pucker. It seemed only natural for Drew to relax around it, slowly but surely allowing the vine to tease inside him, stretching him out lightly and gently. There was a slick lube on it, something the plant must have secreted, and Drew wondered, belatedly, if he should have done more research on the plant. Yet he could not have imagined it would have such intricate husbandry required if it had been sold at the local garden centre.

But maybe it was simply a lucky find, he thought, ducking his head more shyly as the vine slid up under his tail, using that light lubrication to ease inside. It took its time, as if there was no rush at all to the plant, for it knew how to treat its "partners." A massage seemed the least of it as Drew rocked his hips, his shaft sliding out a little more as the pressure under his tail increased. He couldn't stop himself from squeezing

around the vine, even though it seemed to halt the plant
for a moment, as if the plant too was unsure.

"Ah… No… I mean, yes… Yes, you can keep
going…"

He didn't know what he was doing, talking to a
plant that was thrusting into him, pulling back an inch
only to push in further the next time, slowly but surely
working its way deeper and deeper. He shook his head
a little, trying to relieve the tension lining his neck, but
there was only one way relief was to come to him that
day.

He had to let it all loose, grunting and rolling his
shoulders forward, licking his lips, the vine grinding
back and forth. It seemed to thicken, big enough
around that it could have felt like a partner's shaft – and
yet it was better than that still. It twisted and very lightly
curled up inside him in a way no cock could ever do
(well, none Drew had imagined or experienced for
himself) and he heaved for breath, his short claws
digging into the grass and soil.

His tail tried to swing, but the vine had it in such
a loving hold that he instead tightened his grip on it
instead, although he wasn't entirely sure why he
responded in that way. With his cock pushing out, the
vines rubbed along either side of it, grinding up on both
sides of his shaft at the same time, coaxing out every
inch. Drew moaned, blinking, trying to keep his gaze
fixed on the purple bud. Had it softened a little? Ah, he
could not tell, but it was not such a bad thing.

The plant throbbed against his cock and he tried
to look down – but found himself unable. Two vines
snaked around his neck with the tip of one meeting his
lips. It only seemed natural to open his mouth, though
perhaps it was something of a gasp and not an offering
to the vine at all. One vine poking at his lips plunged
inside, though it remained between his teeth, twisting

from side to side in an undulating curve that suggested it was testing the limits of his maw. Afraid of hurting it, even as he salivated too heavily around the vine, he played his slim tongue against the underside, slurping faintly without even considering the consequences of his actions.

The plant seemed to like that, grinding back and forth in his mouth, letting him purse his lips around it to the extent his lips were able to do so. Reptiles had less flexibility there, even dragons, than mammals, but that was something they merely worked with when it came to eating and seducing the pleasures of the body. Drew quivered, a rippling tease rolling through his body, yet he couldn't help himself, as if he had suddenly become greedy when faced with such carnal delights. And he'd only set out that afternoon to do some gardening!

Yet he was taking care of his new favourite plant in the way it needed, the vines teasing around him as his large cock dripped pre-cum. He rolled his hips forward, thrusting without thinking about what he was doing, yet Drew acted on pure instinct. His tongue would have hung out of his mouth if he'd been free to do so, though it was far too busy playing with the vine to even consider such a thing.

It was right, for it could not possibly be wrong, moaning aloud, yet the sound still came out with a muffled softness to it. He groaned instead, shuddering and giving in just a little more to the plant that had, somehow, put him in a kind of bondage without him realising what was going on. The vines had twisted around all four of his legs as he sucked on another, his tail hiked up lewdly for the vine to grind up under his tail. And he needed it all, torn between thrusting into the teasing touch on his cock, making his cock drip over productively, though his arousal swiftly soaked into the grass.

The plant thrust harder, sensing its playmate was growing closer and closer to the edge. Yet it did not need to slow in the slightest, merely testing out the limits of Drew's body and exactly what it needed to get what it needed. It was a massage, quite fairly, but most certainly not the kind of massage the resources had implied. That massage was more what would "get things started" with the greater fun, the plant taking what it craved to be strong and sink its roots deeper. There were nutrients, after all, in semen that could only be gleaned through that manner of play.

Drew would surely find himself more than obliging with his plant in that manner, even if the dragon would find quieter times of day when neighbours were less likely to be awake to enjoy himself. As it was, he moaned wetly around the vine in his mouth as it thrust, mimicking another dragon taking his muzzle, his stomach lurching as something tightened deep within his body.

He needed it – even more as one of the vines opened up to reveal a soft, wet interior, pushing over his cock. He grunted and rocked his hips, trying to hold fast in the moment, but it was not up to the dragon to do so, not in any way. Drew could relax into it, grunting in the back of his throat, a wiggling tease of submission dancing in the back of his mind.

He didn't need to submit, however, as long as both the plant and he were getting what they needed, his grunts mingling with a hum that seemed to vibrate the air itself. It was subtle, however, forcing him to listen hard to pay attention to it, though it didn't matter in the moment. It would end up being just one more thing he would document in his research of the plant, learning more about it than even those who should have been more in the know than him in the online communities. But one had to be truly passionate about their plants to draw on their need like that, though the dragon thrust into the "mouth" of the vine as it swallowed him up, all the same.

Drew was right where he needed to be, cool shade slanting over him as the scent of grass pulled at his nostrils. He tried to close his eyes as the plant sucked around him, his body aching deeply, wanting both climax and the plant's relief at the same time. But he had to keep watching, even as his desire pulled in the pit of his stomach, tightening and demanding he give something to it that he could not.

Only the plant could, for it had Drew in its grasp, sucking and rippling around his cock in a more intimate massage than the dragon could ever have imagined. Drooling and moaning like someone he was not around the vine, the dragon's eyelids fluttered, straining as he quivered on the thrusting vine intent on taking him under his tail. It sped up as the pressure around his cock increased, the pull making him want to drive into it in a more carnal fashion – but, in the end, it was not up to him.

Not as the plant pounded his ass with long, crude strokes, grinding deeper than the drake had ever been penetrated there before. He moaned lewdly, drool splattering from his maw, but Drew did nothing more than revel in it, heat crackling through his form in such a way he couldn't have possibly hoped to hold it back. Within the vine, his shaft throbbed tenaciously, pulsing several times before the eruption swelled through him.

A hot rush of ecstasy poured through his body and he cried out around the vine, need surging through his abdomen. It seemed to roar through far more than just between his thighs, even as the main event came in the throbbing release of his cock. He sent every thick, powerful spurt of cum into the plant as if he was literally trying to pour his seed into it as deeply as was possible, though that was not a concern for any of the partners Drew had been with previously. He just climaxed strongly, feeling the pulse ricochet throughout his entire body, his hind end trying to tuck down as he lost control in the very best of ways.

The plant was there to drink down every last drop of his seed, taking it deep, even as he fed it the semen it needed. He'd later uncover that one climax a week "fed" the plant best – but it might well depend on the plant and require a process of trial and error. But Drew didn't care about any of that in the moment as he grunted and speared his cock in as deep as he could, squeezing *hard* around the vine under his tail as if there was absolutely nothing else for him to focus on in a moment like that.

Ripples of ecstasy flowed through him as he let the plant have him, not a single drop of his seed wasted. Not that Drew would have understood the significance of that at that time, but that was not so bad either. It would all come in time as ripples coursed through him, sweeping over his scales like an unseen hand.

Many unseen hands.

The vines released him slowly as his orgasm tapered off, though they seemed reluctant to let him go. Sliding over his scales, they rubbed and caressed and the dragon imagined they were thanking him for the experience, for he felt he may have given a lot to the plant – while taking so very much more than he could ever have anticipated in return. Drew licked his lips, stretching after the vine as it left his lips, but it only paused for a moment and a kiss as he whimpered.

It was okay. It was just one day, though he still quivered bodily as the vine left his cock, his pink length hard and gleaming with a mixture of cum and the plant's lubrication in the aftermath. He didn't want to let it slide back into his slit yet, his flanks heaving for breath he had not even known he'd needed. Drew's lips tugged into a smile, panting through an open maw, and he chuckled breathlessly, nuzzling in against the purple petals of the plant.

"We...are going to have a lot of fun together."

And so they would. As the massage he'd given his new plant had turned out to be rather more intimate indeed!

Deep in the Cavern

Arlo knew he shouldn't have ventured into the cave alone – everyone was told not to, after all. But the red fox checked the Welsh hills regardless, the route up the mountainside to where the entrance of the cave sat, to ensure he was on a solo expedition. However, the entrance to the tunnel was barely big enough for him to get in without his ears brushing the roof. It opened up inside, however, but the vulpine understood the dangers of such caves more than well enough.

But he couldn't just forget about the monster within. He – well, Arlo had given him the pronoun, without really knowing the gender of the monster he was so drawn to – needed time, needed company. How could anyone live down there in the dark and not crave the warmth of another's touch?

He slipped into the cave with a sigh of relief, dressed comfortably for an even temperature underground. That was one especially nice thing about caving: everything remained an even temperature, when it was insulated with the weight of so much earth around it, rock and the age of the crust of the earth itself seeming to hug its caverns tightly. His tail flicked, the white tip ghost-like in the gloom, though his hind paws were clad in shoes with a good grip on the base, so he would not slip.

The monster's cavern was not too difficult to reach, however, with the light from his helmet dancing and lighting the way before him. Even the smallest movement of his head seemed to send it bouncing all around the walls, casting his eyes over the flatter sheen of rock in some sections, whereas others had been more roughly hewn out.

Not all of the cave system was safe to traverse – and Arlo had no intention of digging into those unsteady zones without company, for he did have a sense of keeping himself safe about him. He wasn't about to do anything too dangerous, always calculating his risks.

Hah, the fox thought, a smile gently tugging at his black lips. *And that's why I stayed with the monster that first time, letting him explore me. That was completely safe, wasn't it?*

But he was only jesting with himself as the cool of the cave encased him, a sense of calm resounding in his chest. Down there, it was not as if he was slipping away from the outside world: he really was cut off from it. There was no mobile phone service, no way for anyone to get in touch with him. He didn't tell anyone when he was heading out there to see his friend, though he was admittedly a very strange kind of friend. If anyone else had known where he was, he would have been able to ask them to call the cave rescue team to check on him, as was standard protocol for most furs who enjoyed dipping underground on such expeditions.

He couldn't risk that. He couldn't risk others finding his rather monstrous friend, despite everything. The fox sighed as he trailed his fingers along one damp wall, marvelling at the feel of the earth around him.

The tunnel opened up into a large cavern, but Arlo crossed it quickly, knowing exactly where he was going. If he ever forgot his way, even though the fox was quite sure that would never happen to him, he would have the luxury of the marks on the walls that he'd left there. They might only have been small scratches in the old slate mine, but the symbols he'd marked there would at least save him if ever required.

Arlo tried to play it safe – so he could throw all that out the window to enjoy himself. A smaller tunnel beckoned him and he followed its twists and turns deep into the belly of the earth, confident in his step as he lit only the path before him. He could have set more lights along the tunnels he frequented, but he wasn't sure if it would have broken the sanctity of it.

Once, the cavern system had been a slate mine – but its time of use as such as long past. Not all of the tunnels had been carved out by anthros either, but by the natural flow of water through the caves, receding, perhaps, after an ice age. It was hard to tell sometimes and even the markers in the rocks, showing different sediments over the course of many, many years, was all down to research and dating.

A low, rumbling groan that had a hint of a growl in it echoed through the cavern and he grinned.

"I'm here."

He said the words quietly, yet they still echoed strangely, like there were many more foxes in there with him, all whispering back to him.

I'm here… I'm here… I'm here… I'm here…

Arlo flicked his tail, nipping at his lip with an edge of shyness, though the cool air on the moisture there drew his attention strangely. It was funny how a little point like that could feel more grounding than even the cast-off slate shifting and rocking under his hind paws, finding a new place to settle while he sought an even step.

Soon enough, however, the tunnel opened up again into a mid-sized cavern where he could just about see the roof with his light if he tipped his head back. A gleaming, dark expanse of water beckoned him, though it could very well have had a threatening aura to it if not for what Arlo knew was down there. Who, after all, would willingly have stepped into pitch-black water without knowing where the bottom was, how deep it was, or what was waiting in there?

The water rippled as he crouched near the edge, his heart pounding. Oh, he knew well enough why he was there, though it always took his breath away as he watched the swathe of gentle tentacles rising from the deep. A curved length broke from the surface and twisted back and forth with a rounded, somewhat narrower tip, reaching for him. The water churned with a further mass of deep purple tentacles, no suckers to be seen, and the monster slid them from the water to teasingly wrap them around the fox.

"Hey!" He laughed, leaning back into them, although they left his clothes swiftly wet, tentacle imprints marking his jacket and trousers. "You're always so friendly… How're you doing down here?"

He was sure the monster understood him, from how those tentacles gently caressed up and under his jaw, tickling against his fur. The fox rocked back on his heels, as much as his body already warmed and he ached to drop to his knees. No… He would let the moment play out a little longer, just so he could better enjoy it, all the time he could spare down there with the monster he had grown to adore.

"I hope you're okay, you seem as active as always."

Arlo chuckled throatily and, slowly, sat back on a rock near the edge of the pool. He suspected the pool was shallow at the edge, though he had never ventured into it, which was more than fair. There was just too much instinct demanding he stay away from the water, while the monster beckoned him with those sinuously twisting tentacles, all winding into and over one another, one organism with a single mind.

The fox curled his fingers around one of the slenderer tentacles, his fingers closing around it, though the tentacle monster already well enough knew what it needed from him. He would be left waddling from the cavern when the monster was done with him, though Arlo's heart leapt in his chest. The back of his mind flickered with guilt for seeking out the monster for his own pleasure too, although it could not be such when the monster came to him each and every time. They got just as much out of their sensual liaison as Arlo did.

"Mmm…"

He murmured to himself as a tentacle twisted into his jacket, the thick, curved length of it heavy against his chest. Ah, it was very much not the time for words, not as far as Arlo was concerned, his breath catching in his throat as he quivered. The tentacles, the finer, smaller ones in the nest of them, wound up against his face and throat, sliding back down to his shoulders to gently ease his hiking jacket from them.

And Arlo allowed it. As much as he didn't want to admit it, he had never had such a sensual experience with anyone other than the tentacle monster. It was as if, down there, there was another, curious presence gently probing at his mind in a way he could lean into, exhaling softly as his lips parted. His tail lifted gently as he perched on the rock that had become theirs, perhaps "their spot," and the fox grunted, shivering as more tentacles brushed over the bare fur of his arms.

Yet the tentacle monster was not at all shy or bashful at all about taking what it wanted from Arlo, eagerly plunging a mid-sized tentacle down the front of his shirt. The fox yelled and laughed, his mirth echoing off the walls of the cavern, though it seemed to spill out over the water as if he had skipped a stone.

"Oh…"

Arlo shuddered bodily, his tail refusing to go back down, giving in slowly. He didn't have to resist in any way, not when he knew he would be well taken care of down there, only… Oh, he didn't know! It just felt like he should have been doing something, something *more*, to help out the tentacle monster, even if they seemed to be doing more than good enough down there. Maybe it was the only life they had, the only life they could live, but the vulpine would be there as often as he could to share in it with them.

He huffed, breath warm against his lips, head tipping back as the tentacles eased up his T-shirt, bit by bit. The soft cotton pulled over his fur, revealing the white of his belly, his arms raising as the tentacle monster curled around his wrists too, helping him out. Of course, Arlo absolutely had a choice in the matter, but it was not as if he would ever have said no, not as his sheath already, wickedly, plumped out ever so faintly with his own arousal. He just couldn't stop his need from swelling, though he would spend hours after the deed relaxing in the nest of tentacles, talking and letting his words flow over the friend who had given him so much already.

His shirt pulled up and over his head, only briefly catching on his snout, but that was easy enough to slip by. The fox exhaled in a puff of breath, though the tentacles worked quickly, deploying some of the thinnest and finest to take care of his trousers. The first few times they'd been together, getting the button undone and zip lowered had been challenging unless Arlo had done it himself, but they had managed. There'd been a few pairs of ripped trousers that the fox had needed to hide when making his way back down the mountain and, of course, to the car park, but the memories made him chuckle.

The button popped free on his trousers and the tentacles scooped under his back and buttocks to help him up from the rock. Pulling his trousers and loose boxers down in one go, the tentacles knew exactly what they were doing as they bared his fur in its entirety, though they had to pause for a moment as they'd forgotten his shoes. Untying the laces took a delicate touch and, as he was raised entirely from the ground, the fox moaned, caressing the tentacles flowing and shifting around him.

"It's okay, it's okay," he murmured, trying his best to reassure them. "I'm here, I'm going to help you out. Please, don't feel like you need to rush."

He wriggled and flexed his foot, doing his best to help his shoes come off, but the monster tossed them aside the moment they were loosened. He moaned, head tipping back further as he was lifted out above the rippling water, tail swinging freely. A tentacle curled around his waist that seemed as thick as his thigh, but the fox held on to more, kissing and nibbling playfully at one that tempted at his lips.

"Mmmm..."

Arlo hummed softly, flicking his tongue out against the tentacle, which was large enough to fill his mouth without straining his jaw too much. There would always be a little strain, however, feeling the muscles pull as he did his best to open his jaws wide, wanting to take as much as the tentacle monster was willing to give him.

The tentacle bopped his nose and he licked his lips as it teased own over his upper lip and gently slid over his tongue, easing into his mouth. It pressed his tongue into the base of his mouth, between the lines of his teeth, yet the fox was not concerned at all about hurting the tentacle. He'd been wary, at first, of nipping it accidentally, but any accidental grazes with his teeth had only made the monster quiver deliciously, not a mark left on any of the tentacles at all.

It was exquisite to have his mouth filled like that, his body not at all in contact with the ground as his arms were bound once more and pulled up restrictively behind his head. He didn't need them and yet it seemed the monster was feeling in more dominant, possessive mood that day, forcing him to bend to their will. Arlo twisted beautifully, arching his back and doing his best to drive his hips forward.

He moaned, letting himself be lost in the moment, his head tipping down so his legs were held higher, by the monster, than his torso. The angle didn't bother the fox in the slightest, his legs parted with one lightly bent, his body no more than a toy for the monster to do with as they pleased. Arlo grunted, playing his tongue around the tentacle, although he tried to pull his lips tightly around it, sucking. That was harder than it should have been when he wanted to suck and keep his jaws parted widely, an anthro muzzle not quite designed for the subtleties of delivering mind-blowing oral.

But they managed. They always found a way for pleasure to rise through, even as his sheath swelled and the red tip of his cock protruded, bit by bit, making itself known. It had to push its way out sooner or later, but the tentacles had something else in mind right then and there.

A tentacle opened wide, parting in four petal-like shapes as it swallowed up his cock as soon as it appeared. His sheath tugged around his length as it emerged and, still, all the fox could do was twist and rock lightly within the grasp of the tentacles, luxuriating in the moment. A low groan rose from him, however muffled it was around the tentacle stuffing his maw, though he still tried to play his tongue around it, sweeping over the smooth, lightly textured length as he drooled.

The tentacle sucking his cock into its "mouth" pulled and rippled, swiftly coaxing out more and more of his member. His shaft ached deliciously and he moaned again, eyelids fluttering, though keeping his eyes open and fixed on the wonderfully writhing mass was harder than he could have imagined. Arlo bucked his hips, need getting the better of him, but more thick tentacles wound around his legs, one knee bent while they kept him completely locked in place.

That didn't stop more tentacles still from crawling over his body, his cock aching within the tight, slick hold. As tentacles pushed over him, brushing his fur in the wrong direction and then smoothing it back down once more, the fox tried to spear his shaft into the tentacle, wanting more, craving more. There was simply something about the monster that called on that baser need inside him, what snarled and heaved and moaned for debauchery, lust, pounding on to the exclusion of all else.

The cave didn't exist for him anymore, not in any way that should or could have had meaning to the vulpine. The water splashed and rippled lightly around the tentacle monster, though they had a way of moving through the water that seemed like they were one with it, barely disturbing the surface – unless they had reason to. There was a sense of deliberateness about their rippling pull and swathe, even how they gently brushed over the front of the fox's throat, teasing over his Adam's apple.

The cave walls were above, but, of course, his helmet had been long set aside. A tentacle had guided it to the rock on which he had been sitting, so it cast a manufactured shaft of light across the watery cavern. It was not all that much to see by, though it still helped slightly illuminate the dark purple tentacles, how they twisted before him, rising like a wall of trees or perhaps kelp, caught by the flow and pull of the elements.

It was better still as his head tipped to the side and he caught the dancing shadows flickering on the wall behind the monster, above the surface of the water. The shadows seemed to play with their own shape, winding in and out of one another, as if maybe there were two sensual creatures there, not just the one Arlo returned to, time after time again. His eyes flickered closed again, though he was far from tired, not as the tentacle pulled and sucked around his cock, encasing his full length and the, as yet, unformed knot. It would not affect anything at all with the tentacle monster, of course, if his knot swelled too soon, but he might have multiple orgasms as a result of it.

Even then, Arlo did not know for how long he would enjoy his time in the tentacle monster's cavern, his cock twitching within its hot, wet grasp. He didn't even comprehend, after all that time, just how the tentacle could be hot as well; he would have anticipated the monster's body being cold-blooded, but things like that truly were hard to say. The fox tried to twist, his fur lightly damp, but he was held tightly in a grasp that didn't yet need to release him.

With a moan, he tensed his quads, squeezing his glutes briefly, a tentacle probing under his tail. It wanted more from him that day than just his cock and Arlo was more than happy to allow the monster access, doing his best to relax his anal ring. Little things like that could be harder than ever, however, when all his body ached to do was to buck and moan on a tentacle that felt like it was stretching right up into the core of his body, plunging as deep as it was possible to go.

Still, he managed to ease the clenching of his pucker enough for the tentacle to wriggle inside, slimmer right at the tip and then rapidly thickening up to a meaty girth that had Arlo swooning. The fox grunted, drooling, and tried to rock his hips back on to it, yet the monster knew just how much he could take. Working him open steadily, the tentacle ground back and forth as he shivered into the tantalising touch, his anal ring easing wider around the girth.

"Ohhhh…"

His cry was muffled, but that didn't at all stop it from spilling from his lips, his lower abdomen aching in a warming way. Need spread through him, skin prickling all the way down to the tips of his fingers and his toes, the fox rocking his hips weakly from side to side. Yet the tentacle beast restricted his range of motion even then, squeezing firmly around his wrists and pulling back, wrenching mildly at his shoulders.

The moan the fox gave in response to that was utterly salacious, tail twitching even though there was a tentacle grinding its length up against the underside, preventing him from lowering it again. No, they didn't want Arlo's tail to at all get in the way as he was fucked, the tentacle grinding back and forth passionately within his tail hole.

Arlo whined, the overload of sensation getting to him. From the tentacles sliding over his form and the squeeze of those gripping his lips to the raunchy drive of the one plunging into his ass, the fox could do nothing. And it was that very restriction that allowed him to let go just a little bit more, exulting in the moment rather than allowing overstimulation to consume him. His cock throbbed, pulsing hotly with a rush of blood within the tentacle, though it held fast at the base of his cock. In his position, the fox blinked up the length of his body, still with his head tipped down, catching sight of his shaft for a few moments.

The tentacle sucking down his cock rippled with the pulsating massage, though he swore he could feel a strange, trembling vibration coursing into his dick too. It even resounded into his balls, though those largely went untouched by the tentacle monster, his hips bucking helplessly in its thrall. He was where he needed to be and yet he knew he was just a toy, a plaything, his need searing at the forefront of his mind despite everything.

Around his cock, the tentacle squeezed, as if an unseen paw was manipulating it from the outside – and then more tentacles filled his vision so he couldn't even see the shadows shifting on the wall anymore, locked down in the moment. The tentacles blocked his vision and most light from reaching his eyes, but he was fine right where he was. Even as the tentacle under his tail sped up, his passage clenching roughly around it, though it was not as if he could do anything at all at that point to force it from him if it was too much.

He wanted it all, greedily sucking around the tentacle like a whore, losing every last inhibition that may have rested too heavily on his shoulders, weighing him down. Such inhibitions had never belonged there anyway and the fox shrugged them off with a muffled yelp, his own saliva slick on his lips.

Yet his knot swelled, betraying his own need. It pushed urgently out against the tentacle sucking around it and he whined with a roll of his eyes as it pulsed behind his knot, as if the tentacle itself was joining in with "tying" them together. He grunted again and tried to rock his hips, yet the fox could barely even tell whether he was thrusting or not, moving at all, with the mass of tentacles constricting even lightly around his chest.

In the mass of tentacles, pleasure lanced through him, demanding he pay attention to it at all costs, that there was simply no other option there. His back arched mildly and he squeezed passionately around the tentacle in his ass, like he was trying to break free and yet grind on to at the same time. Such opposing actions were normal to a confused mind, overwhelmed by sensation and languishing so very deeply in emotion, heaving and panting through his nostrils alone as ecstasy swelled.

He groaned and tried to yowl brokenly, yet there was little warning as the pressure increased around his cock, losing more pre-cum than ever into the tentacle's hungry "maw." Arlo thrust brokenly, the tentacles moving right along with him, though he was only aware of his hips moving by the tentacles shifting with him, adding to the lustful lurch of his body. His inner thigh on the right burned from the strain of keeping his legs apart, but Arlo would have not had it any other way as he moaned lewdly and let it all course through him, the heated swell of orgasm impossible to deny.

His hips jerked and he tried to suck even harder around the tentacle, just for something to focus on, as his cock erupted. Arlo had never been one to cum that hard when he was just having fun himself, but the tentacle monster changed all of that for him. Every throb around his cock had him spending more and more cum into it, feeling like his orgasm was going on forever, a heated swathe of bliss drowning him, as if he was just about to be pulled under the surface of the water, never again to return.

The fox knew where he belonged, however, and he swam through the hazy delight with a weak grunt, head spinning with an overload of pleasure. There was too much stimulation around his cock, but that was something he was already more than used to as the tentacle monster would not let him go until it was, finally, good and done with him.

That could be minutes. That could be hours. It had never been longer than that – but the fox would have stayed down there for day after day, if the opportunity had been offered to him. To be nothing more than something for the tentacle monster to empty its load into was all he craved.

And yet...that was not quite what was to happen that day, no. His ass squeezed around the lustful intrusion under his tail and he groaned openly, saliva dripping from his lips, the tentacle before him glistening with a sheen of his own drool. It sped up, though the sucking tentacle eased off ever so slightly, which was unusual for that one. The tentacle wriggled deeper still up into his tail hole, thickening somewhat, and desire lurched in the pit of his belly all over again.

Something was different and he still craved it, the butterflies of anticipation fluttering in his stomach as his heart rate seemed to quicken all over again. He rocked his hips, keen for it, though he could not have expected the lustful ripple that coursed through every single tentacle at once. If he thought the tentacle monster was a part of the water it lived in, perhaps he was a part of the monster too, just another appendage it could use exactly as it pleased.

He rather liked that thought, but something large pushing up against his anal ring dragged his attention harshly back into the present. Arlo grunted and closed his eyes tight, straining through the moment as his pucker was stretched far wider than it ever had been before. Something big pushed insistently into his ass through the tentacle and he exhaled in a hot rush of breath as something rounder with a smaller, narrower end ground into his anal passage.

An egg...

The fox bucked lightly and groaned, yet Arlo was prey to the tentacles, unable to do anything else at all as he rolled his lips lightly and succumbed to the tentacle monster. The egg worked its way deep up inside him, although it was swiftly followed by another. Where it may have harmed his body, it did nothing of the sort but left a warming glow spreading through him, a low grunt in the back of his throat. One, two, three, four – and five – eggs teased into him, each one forcing his pucker wide as he squirmed on it.

Dimly, Arlo was aware of the need to orgasm all over again, working his lips and tongue against the smooth length just resting in his maw. His cock ached and throbbed, but it was the stimulation under his tail that made him want to squirm and moan all the more, dazed and wanton with a flare of lust anything like what he'd experienced before. Arlo groaned, his tail flicking weakly, yet the soft fluff only brushed up against more tentacles, the writhing mass impossible to escape.

Two more eggs, one after the other, travelled down the length of the tentacle in his ass, the swell of them obvious through its stretched "skin," if it could even be called such. He swallowed hard, eyelashes fluttering, and whimpered weakly as his backside was stretched again.

The strain was glorious, making him feel as if he wasn't going to be able to take it, that it was going to be too much – and yet he held it, the egg sliding into him past the widest point at the last possible moment. His ass wiggled, squeezing around the intrusion when he really should have relaxed, but instinct and the needs of his body were not always on his side.

With the tentacles covering him completely, from head to paw, he let himself be enveloped, lost, for a while, to anything other than bliss. He moaned, though there was no one there to bear witness to it, the monster laying eight and then nine eggs into his ass. As the final egg, the tenth one, ground up under his tail, the biggest of them all, he moaned out a smothered cry with a jerky, biting orgasm, his prostate milked with every egg until he could bear it no more. The exultant ecstasy was there for Arlo to take and the fox would have been a fool not to snatch it all up for himself.

So, he laid there, comfortable in the realisation that he was going to be down in the cavern for quite some time, though that was far from a bad thing. With a gentle, slithering caress running all over his body, teasing under his arms and turning him so they were the highest point once again, the tentacle monster rumbled a low, crooning cry to him too, joining him in his verbal lust.

As the last egg settled inside him, his abdomen grossly swollen with the lump filling of eggs, the fox hung in the tentacles, twitching in the afterglow. His cock spent weak spurts of cum into the tentacle-maw, but it was there to suck on him for as long as it was needed. And there was still more passion to come between them, the tentacles squirming encouragingly, his eyelids fluttering apart once more.

Deep in the cavern, both fox and tentacle monster reaped all they craved from one another, all in the very best of ways.

A Fine Feline

"Hm… This could be fun."

Jon laid back on the bed, the silver tabby cat's leg hanging off the side as if to raise his leg to the mattress would take far too much energy entirely. He didn't have long hair growing at the top of his head like some furs, but only his natural fur, keeping it as well-groomed as any feline furs tended to. Wearing only a loose pair of boxer briefs on his slim, lithe frame, he tapped the app open on his phone with a gleam in his eye, having only just installed it.

Jon's bedroom was familiar around him, though his bed was already coming unmade with the duvet tugging out slowly from under his favourite, comfortable pillow. He rolled over as he twisted, though never on to his front, holding on to his phone despite his changes in position. A shelf held books, though there were more still on a small bookcase at the wall opposite the foot of his bed, with a TV on top of it. Not being home all that much with work and life, the early-twenties cat didn't see much point in upgrading, regardless of how he liked to watch films too.

But he was home then and boredom ached through him, the curtains of his bedroom closed against the dark of the night, his flat warm in the late summer air. It was the perfect weather for him to sprawl in, yet the itch to do something nagged at him, scanning through the app.

"Tentacle…companion… Just click here?"

Jon sighed and eyed it suspiciously, eyes darting away from the phone to his bedroom door, though he lived alone. Still, the notion of never quite being left alone was a hangover from his further studies and some time working away, sleeping in a dorm. At least he had always had his own room, but it was still difficult, or so he felt, to gain some sense of privacy there.

The cat was alone there, at the very least, and he tapped into the chosen companion with the pad of his first finger. His tail flicked back and forth, need getting the best of him, though he was ever so slightly wary of the app not being paid for. The "sexy companions," even with a magical edge to them that came through even in standard, everyday tech, usually were charged, but maybe it was a free trial.

Pawing over his inner thigh, he pulled his fingers up slowly over the front of his boxers, nipping at the inside of his cheek as they drew over his sheath. He shook his head and accepted the user agreement regardless of his trepidation, for there didn't seem to be anything of ill note there at all.

Jon twitched, pushing his hips up from the bed as something tingled through him and he set the phone down on the bed between his legs. It had been a long time since he'd tried a tentacle companion for fun, but he was more than ready for it as he gripped the bedsheets with both hands, his short claws digging in where they were not retracted. His tail, however, still lashed back and forth between his legs as the screen of his phone glowed and, slowly, six tentacles rose from it.

It was as if they were simply entering his reality through a portal, though Jon was more than comfortable enough with little flickers of magic just like that. Maybe he didn't see much use for them when he wasn't looking for something beyond his reality, though the feline still squirmed and rocked his hips down, not even bothering to move his underwear. His narrow chest heaved for breath, lips tugging in a smile, and he rocked his hips from side to side as the blue-hued, tapered tentacles wriggled up his legs.

Around and around and around… They enwrapped his legs, twisting and twining their way up from his hind paws all the way up to his thighs. Squeezing, they tempted at parting his legs a little further and the flexible feline allowed it all to happen, though Jon was not all that sure how that was to play out. How far would the tentacles go with him? There was magic, but sometimes such limits were unsure.

But he relaxed into that as much as he could, the tentacles so far avoiding his tail as they snaked up his body, trapping his torso and winding around him. Two of the thickest plunged deviously into his boxers and Jon let out a subtle yowl as he rolled his hips up, keep to have them brushing over his sheath and between his legs, teasing over his balls.

"Oh... Ohhh, yesss..."

At least he didn't seem to have anything at all to worry about with those tentacles, huffing and panting as he licked his lips and the tentacles wrenched his legs so wide he was nearly doing the splits. The boxers pulled up against his crotch, but the tentacles didn't see that as a problem, bulging to tear straight through the fabric.

"Ah!"

He cried out, wriggling as the tentacles slithered around him, though there seemed to be very little of his body that was in contact with the bed anymore, a huge, bulky length of tentacle that he could not see the end of ensnaring him. Jon's eyelids half-closed, letting himself sink there, his cock swelling into his sheath. The lightly barbed (not sharply so) length pushed out eagerly and some of the smaller tentacles, the more delicate ones, rubbed against it, toying with the softer, more pliable barbs with thick bases, seeing just how they would react.

He moaned and rocked his hips, the tentacles grasping his wrists and finally pinning them up above his head, between the pillows on his bed. Jon tried to thrust, yet he didn't even seem to have that agency over his body, a tentacle probing at his lips. He hesitated for a fraction of a second before opening up for it and the tentacle rubbed against his lips before sliding inside, as if it was being considerate of his feelings and ability to take it into his mouth.

That was nice of it, but he languished there, rocking his hips lightly, all to the extent he was able. His cock pushed out insistently until the entire length was on show, throbbing a little, though the sensation of such little pulses was so subtle that it wasn't actually visible – no matter what spicy, erotic readings might have tried to say. At least, it was not obvious on his frame: but Jon was not a fur with a particularly large member that may have had more blood surging through it to fuel an erection.

It didn't matter, not as he sucked lightly on the tentacle in his mouth, enjoying how the slender tip flicked back and forth, exploring the limits of his body. Something wet pressed up under his tail, but, with so many tentacles wrapping him up – the length of them all made it seem like there was far more than six curled around him – he couldn't tell just which one it was. And he didn't need to either, not as the tentacle produced its own slick lubrication. He would have bucked against it, but all the feline could do was thrash his tail, sweeping the curl of it back and forth, as the tentacles left it free.

His cheeks bulged as the tentacle in his mouth thrust back and forth, grinding over his tongue and plumping up to the perfect size to stretch his lips and jaw a little more. Jon tried to mew, a soft cry, yet it was muffled by that tentacle, drooling around it as his lips and the tendril grew slicked with his saliva with every passing second.

Yet his attention zeroed in on the tentacle probing at his ass, teasing up inside him slowly, spreading him open in a lewd, wet gape. The lubrication helped the tapered tip pop inside as he groaned, eyes closed, letting himself revel in every sensation as if the outside world did not matter in the slightest.

Raised from the bed, the tentacles writhed and pulled around him, the shifting, dragging pressure of them clawing at his senses. He tried weakly to flick his tongue against the tentacle, but even that seemed to elude him, as if he was a passive player in his own ecstasy. Jon's hips rocked, but it didn't seem like it was him thrusting, not really, but the tentacles controlled him, the thick one bearing up into his tail hole to strain his pucker open wider and wider.

The feline took it all hungrily, his cock throbbing – ah, but the tentacles didn't pay any attention to that. No matter how much he squirmed and wriggled, he couldn't get the tentacles to give him more than a fleeting touch there, the remains of his ruined boxers on the bed under him. Yet it was as if the cat was floating, the tentacles swaying and rocking him, rippling along his form as his fur was flattened to his body.

His ears twitched, one of the few parts of his body that were left to him, that he could move. His tail flicked, but it didn't bring him any relief in the slightest as he tried to get something, anything, on his barbed length with the narrower tip. But it was the tentacle grower fatter and firmer under his tail that clawed at his attention the most, stretching him out as it worked back and forth in a rippling push and shove, giving him the rougher, more demanding strokes he craved.

Jon didn't worry too much about how the tentacle knew he liked that, but he didn't have to worry. He didn't even have to think about in the slightest as he languished there, heat rising to his cheeks and crawling down his neck in a prickling pull. The pressure under his tail, however, was immense, making him want to bear down against it, even though clenching his ass wouldn't help him out at all.

The friction, however, dragged at his attention, giving him a rhythm and a push he could focus on, despite everything. He moaned aloud and drooled around the tentacle, though at least having his maw stuffed meant Jon could stay quieter than he usually was with a partner. Did the tentacles count as a partner? Oh, the cat didn't have it in himself to care!

The rippling pull of the tentacles over his body was too alluring to ignore, almost like a full body massage but very much not one he suspected he would ever be able to get at any spa. His soft fur clung to him a little more tightly as the tentacles secreted a little more of that lubrication, though it left the tentacles lightly sticking to him all over, as if it aided them in gripping him.

I've never thought of tentacles like this before…

He groaned and let them rock his body, leaning into the pushing rhythm of the tentacle grinding into his ass. He tried to push back against them, but there was only so much he could do there, submitting to the gripping beauty of it. Even though the tentacles secreted some manner of sticky lube that affected his fur different to his tail hole, it was not at all an uncomfortable sensation, merely letting the tentacles squeeze around him. It vaguely reminded Jon of a serpent's tail, but he leaned into it with a grunt and a huff, an aching need pulling through the pit of his belly.

Oh, how he had to cum, his cock feeling like a throb of blood was pulsing through it, his length harder and more sensitive than ever before. As much as he grunted, however, still nothing came, so he was forced to twist anxiously against the cool of the room tingling over his member.

It should have been a crime for his cock to feel that sensitive, like he would blow his load at a moment's notice, yet he was not quite given that pleasure he needed. His tail flicked back and forth, dangling out from the twisting tentacles, but the cat had to hold on there, his chin tucking down ever so slightly as he tried his best to feel everything coursing through him, needing it more than ever.

The pulse of the tentacles around him, not shifting from his fur but squeezing tighter and tighter.

How the tentacle shoving into his ass flexed before the push.

The brush of air over his cock, pre-cum dripping, beading and falling thickly from the tip.

Even the tightness of a collar-like tentacle around his throat, locking him in there and letting him know, undoubtedly, there was no escape to be had for him.

He didn't want to escape, no. He just wanted to be there, luxuriating in it all, heaving and panting, dragging in what breath he could throw his nostrils as his tail twitched weakly. Jon had always needed stimulation to his cock to climax, for that just seemed to be how his body was built, but it just wasn't there for him. The tentacles stripped him of even the ability to take that for himself, huffing and grunting, licking the tendril in his mouth desperately for any form of relief.

It was worse than being edged – even better, perhaps. He'd never quite be able to quantify in his mind just how two things could be true at the same time, but Jon would not deny it. He heaved for breath and tried to keep his eyes open, straining to take in all the visual stimulation he could too, all so he could, maybe, somehow, get off.

But his cock only throbbed, no matter how hard he stared longingly at the tentacles throbbing with wicked pulses around him, the cat's body still held aloft from the bed. The sheen of the light catching them was purely hypnotic as he wriggled and twisted, luxuriating in it all and yet whimpering throatily around the stuffing in his maw. He wouldn't have been able to put into words how the tentacles bubbled and tremored as they fucked him, but no one was there to ask him about the experience anyway. Even his phone was hidden, at the point where they'd all emerged, tucked away where it was not needed for the time being.

Maybe next time, Jon could record. However, he knew with full certainty that he was definitely going to be calling on the tentacles again, even if there ended up being a charge for the kinky app.

It was all worth it as pleasure rolled through him, over and over again, in time with every single thrust. Jon tongued the tentacle in his maw, pursing his lips around the it, though he didn't have much room to move, the restraint glorious as he struggled against it just to feel how tight the bonds were. There was nothing more exquisite to him, not even able to take a full, even breath with the tentacles seductively encasing his chest.

He wondered, dimly, cock throbbing, if they would take him with them when the timer on the app ran out, dragging him back into the phone – or wherever they'd come from. That would not be such a bad thing, even if he might be forever teetering on the edge of pleasure, rocking and aching for bliss that would never quite come.

He may have enjoyed that, despite the lust trembling through him. But he was not to be denied as the tentacles brushed against his cock finally, almost as if his member was a complete afterthought. There was no ceremony to it as two twined around his length much as they had done his body, legs still wrenched far apart as the tentacles caressed his shaft and pumped the length.

"Mmm-hmm-mmph!"

Jon bucked and moaned, even though the cat didn't get very far, not even as pleasure lanced sharply through him, refusing to let the feline even think about or consider anything else at all. Locked into the moment that would not release him, he howled brokenly around the tentacle, which was slick with his drool, but he couldn't help it. He was where he needed to be and the surge of pleasure, his cock even too sensitive at that moment, but he held on through it all.

Need billowed through him and he yowled once more, tail swinging within the tentacle's hold, but his cock was already spurting long ropes of cum. His mind took another moment to catch up with the shock of pleasure as it gripped him, every muscle in his body seemingly going tense at once. Jon's vision whited out, forgetting even to breathe (if only for a few lost moments) as bliss swamped him, dragging him under with the tentacles twining around him, loving sliding and coursing over his body again as his body sank to the bed.

He convulsed, bucking and thrusting, the relaxed tentacles finally allowing that. Yet the ease of movement came too late for him, as Jon barely even noticed. His fingers twitched and he sucked hard on the filling in his mouth, losing himself there as more and more cum arced from him, painting the tentacles pouring over him.

The bliss was worth it, coming to his high at just the right time as the tentacles retreated. The timer was up and they withdrew, slowly, back to the phone, winding up back to wherever the magic took them.

Maybe that was something Jon would understand one day, but it really wasn't necessary for his kind of fun.

He could lay there, fingers tracing the lines of the tentacles as they all slid from his body, teasing from his panting lips and slowing pulling from his tight backside. Jon huffed, dragging in breath, cock still spurting weaker strings of cum, which marked his lower abdomen and the point at the top of his thighs.

"Huh… Mmm… Uh…"

Jon tried to form words, but they didn't come – or not as easily as he wanted them to. With a wiggle of his hips, he grunted as the tentacle tip finally slipped from his ass, leaving his hole lewdly gaping, just slightly so. It was enough for him as he laughed breathlessly and slumped back into the bed, the mattress feeling so very soft after his tight, sticky attention.

He would definitely use the app again…but, first, he needed to recover from that round. A cat, after all, had to have everything their heart desired.

Even if it was just some kinky self-pleasure to bring a smile to their lips at the end of a long day.

A Dragon of the Deep

Morred's small boat skipped over the waves, bouncing in a spray of white foam as he directed it in a straight line, the choppy ocean making his task more difficult than usual. Heading out to a small island off the south-east English coast that had no name, as only those who were not looking for it could find it, he smiled. Others, surely, got lost all the time and found the island – well, maybe not all the time. But they had never been able to find their way back like he had, as they had not met Nerin out there.

The dragon never felt as alive as he did out in the water, sea spray marking his green scales, though he was a dragon who may have been more typically found in the air than on the ground, or even out in the ocean. With large wings with a pale green membrane stretched between the powerful spines, he could easily take flight and soar through the sky, but he was happier out on the ocean, his head held high and looking to the horizon.

Oh, the sea was such an enigma, even as the island came into view. His long tail balanced him, though it was not so long that it was the kind of tail that wanted to twist and curl back and forth: more of a weighty, steadying tail. It was thick at the root, the scales protective and chunky, but they matched the wider plate-scales running down his front, offering a blue-green hue that offset the green of the rest of his scales. Morred's horns were small and neat, with a subtle change of direction midway down the length, though they barely extended back beyond his skull.

He kept his wings folded in against his back when he was out there, for expanding them may well have thrown his little speedboat off course, but he was nearly where he needed to go. Out there, amongst a cluster of rocks rising from the ocean as if they wanted to be an island, he would find them: the creature of the deep.

Well, Nerin was more than that, though Morred liked to tease him. He slowed the boat, cutting the engine and dropping the anchor when he got to the right spot, waiting. There was no rush, for Nerin would find him, though it was Morred too who had given Nerin his name, for the ocean-dwelling drake had not had one in a language or tongue Morred could understand.

Sea dragons, after all, of Nerin's species, had their own language, though he was fortunate enough that he spoke English too. Chatting with Morred had offered the dragon a wider vocabulary too and, when Nerin was willing to come in to land, resting in a rock pool or similar, they watched films on an old, portable DVD player. Morred would have brought his laptop, but there was more of a problem with internet signal off in remote areas and, of course, the DVD player was something he wouldn't mind losing if it got accidentally splashed with salt water.

He hoped Nerin would come in to land at some point, however, when he went out to the little cabin with the pine trees bordering it, nearly right on the shore front. It was remote and the type of small cabin that he was lucky enough to have use of but had to hike to, which made helping with maintenance a little troublesome. However, his uncle appreciated any assistance he could get and rarely managed to make the trip out to the cabin on his land. Being on the mainland, it was still a risk that they could be discovered there, but it was still far enough in the backwoods that they would be safer.

Morred leaned over the edge of the boat, the dragon's heavy tail balancing him.

"Nerin? Are you out there?"

He swayed back and forth, trying to peer down into the water, but the sea dragon was not going to let him see him coming. Morred should have expected the light touch on his left shoulder, one of Nerin's slithering tentacles sliding over it, though he still jumped and spun about, rocking the boat as his heart leapt and thudded in his chest.

"Jeez, Morred!"

He swore under his breath, but there was still a laugh in his tone, the drake not really mad at Nerin at all. The sea dragon raised his head out of the water, eyes gleaming darkly as the irises shrank where they no longer needed to take in as much light as possible to see in the deeper water.

"You always get me," Morred laughed, though he pulled his T-shirt off as he spoke, scales prickling eagerly, his body aching to join his friend… Or perhaps Nerin was really more than a friend. "Why do you have to sneak up on me every time though?"

The sea dragon shrugged and rolled his shoulders back, although there was still a smile pulling at his damp lips. Unlike Morred, Nerin had smooth skin like that of a dolphin and his body was shorter, a little more close-coupled. Fronds swept around him that reminded Morred of a sea dragon – not like Nerin, of course, or other types of sea dragon, but the much smaller fish that was a leafy seadragon, which was a member of the pipefish family. They blended in with swaying kelp as they clung to it, seeking out tiny morsels of prey in the ocean.

He had similar fronds draping from his body, flowing from his neck, his shoulders, even his limbs too. The fronds stretched out from his back, following the line of his spine all the way down his tail, where they waved and danced out from his tail too, in all directions, making it look larger than it was. In a sense, they provided a bit of drag in the water so he was not the quickest of sea creatures, but he was much better able to blend in with his environment, waiting and lurking. The dark blue and green of them dappled through, breaking up the outline so they were harder to see.

Nerin's tentacles were better concealed and mostly tucked under the fronds, all sprouting from the sides of his back, up close to his spine where the spinous processes ended, so muscles and ligaments streamed up into them and they could act without tugging too much on his spine. Morred, however, had worked out quite early on that just using a single tentacle affected the oceanic dragon's balance and position in the water – which was fascinating from an anatomical perspective.

But he didn't have the heart to dig into things at that time, not quite like that, his heart suddenly pulling with longing for Nerin. He held out his hands to Nerin and the sea dragon flowed up seamlessly into the boat with him, using his tail and the sinuous push of his body, moving somewhat like a cross between a dolphin and a serpent, helping him ascend that distance.

Sometimes, words were not needed and Morred clung to Nerin as if nothing else in the world could change things between them, his heart hammering and tears prickling in the corners of his eyes. It had been too long since they were together and the drake urgently pushed against him too, pressing in so hard that Morred shuddered at the feel of Nerin's heart beating against him.

Ah. So, at least they were on the same page, though Nerin swallowed hard, his nostrils puckering and pulling as he inhaled Morred's scent. The drake smelled of land but there was a muskier scent there too, something that Nerin could not otherwise locate out in the ocean. Salt layered everything out there, but there were crisper, fresher scents to be found there too, filtering through the undercurrent of the ocean to sense what was around him. Even the taste in the water of a fish in distress could be enough to draw his attention from up to two miles away. He was not as honed in that sense as some sharks were, but his methods of hunting down his next fishy meal were much more refined than even those predators.

But Nerin allowed those thoughts to slip from his mind in the moment, easing away on the current. He rocked his hips back and forth, his forelegs clinging to Morred's shoulders, wishing he had something he could say that would make it better, to somehow convey just how he longed for Morred every minute that the two of them were apart.

"I...missed you."

That didn't do it, but Morred squeezed him a little tighter. Nerin exhaled, his raised nostrils puckering, but he needed more. They would have time to talk later, perhaps sprawled out in the bottom of the boat, rocked gently on the waves, but he needed that closeness, that intimacy.

Nerin's nose trailed down Morred's cheek and neck as the dragon's breath hitched lightly, though the sea dragon had pushed his slender, serpent-like body up against Morred when he stood. His tentacles brushed free of his suddenly heavy fronds, but he had more at his disposal than just his finned feet and his maw.

"Ah, Nerin..."

Morred grunted, but the dragon didn't stop Nerin as the sea drake nuzzled down, his tentacles sweeping around the sea dragon. They snuggled around his torso, hugging his waist, and Morred leaned back gratefully into them, accepting the support. Even when they twisted up under his shirt and gently into his shorts, not yet brushing anything overly sensitive: Nerin was more than able to make himself clear, warbling softly as he shivered against his partner.

He would tell Morred later of his plans to move to an island further along the coast, where it was easier to get a boat out too, though it would be up to the land dragon (well, land and sky dragon) to sort out planning permissions for building a home there. It was what they had been hoping for, together, but it took time to pull something like that together. Until then, maybe his cabin would suffice at least for a little more time together: a break from reality of a sort.

Morred exhaled as Nerin drew him down to the side of the boat, tipping it to the side even though it was a little bit of a risky move. He raised his arms to let Morred draw his T-shirt up and over his head, the cool ocean breeze licking at his bared scales. Yet Morred would not be cool for long as heat prickled through him, as if lines of sensation were following the edges of each and every scale on his body, hips rolling forward with subtle, sensual need.

"Nerin…" He breathed, licking his lips, the drake bobbing up to kiss his lips briefly — but it was no more than a chaste peck that time. "You always seem to be in tune with me."

Nerin grinned, twisting more tentacles around Morred as the dragon pulled down his shorts, tugging his underwear along with them. Nerin was quick to make sure Morred was as naked as he was, for Nerin, of course, did not naturally need or want to wear clothing. He had more of a feral body-type — and that was yet another conflict in traditional fur society, even when it came to dragons.

"Mmm…yes," he admitted quietly, his tail drifting back and forth, but it hung low with the weight of the fronds draping from it. "But I miss you. And I know the flow of your air currents, as you know the flow of my oceanic currents."

The comparison did not quite work, though it was not the time for Morred to speak more freely about how the air moved. It was easier to lean into the moment as the slit at his abdomen parted, allowing the pale blue of his cock-tip out into the air.

Yet it was not allowed a moment in which to breathe and for Morred to rest there, not as those tentacles, thick around with an almost swollen, defined, oval head to each of them, swept up alongside his cock. Two meaty tentacles pulled up the length on either side and swept down, every pumping tease of them coaxing out another sliver of his meat until the full eight-inches were out and throbbing faintly in the cool air. Morred sucked in a breath, ever so slightly light-headed, but Nerin's tentacles swept and pulled over him, locking them together into a kiss once more.

Nerin was not idle as his own member pushed out, for their bodies were designed in quite a similar manner when it came to their genitalia. He too had a slit for his shaft and internally held testes, but his cock was longer still, reaching twelve-inches with a light undulation to the length. The tip twisted back in the opposite direction to the thick, girthy root of his shaft, the slit almost tight around the base of his cock. It tugged lightly, but Nerin paid it no mind as his tentacles pushed up between his legs, curling around and up his thighs.

"Mmmph…"

Morred grunted, the drake pulled closer and closer to the edge of the boat. It rocked and tipped dangerously, but a tentacle still teased up under his tail all the same. That was a little more difficult for Morred as it pushed up against the underside of his tail and prodded at his pucker, gently applying increasing pressure. It would be harder, however, for Nerin to penetrate him while they were in the water – for that was exactly where they were heading – so they had to initiate that while out of the water.

The dragon gasped and leaned into Nerin, the dragon dropping a little lower, but still letting his tentacles wind up and caress Morred's face and neck. They slid tenderly along the sides of his muzzle and he followed them with his lips, not quite knowing in which direction to look, although Nerin would soon enough take care of that for him, Morred had no concern at all about that.

He rocked back lightly, his tail lifted, though there was a tentacle winding around it, pulling it up higher so his ass was completely exposed. Morred shivered, the ripple running through his whole body as his wings rustled against his back, but he didn't try to pull away. It was just briefly overwhelming to have so many sensations colliding all at once, his attention drawn down to his cock and back again to the steady stretch and penetration under his tail.

"You're tighter than usual..."

Nerin nuzzled into his chest and slid down his belly, nipping playfully at Morred's scales. He shook his head and swallowed hard, for his tentacles were overly sensitive and tactile too – perhaps even more so than the skin on the rest of his body. His shaft throbbed, dripping a stream of pre-cum, but his tentacle ground a little deeper into Morred's tail hole, stretching him out slowly. With only two inches pushed up into the dragon's ass, he pulled back, gasping in pleasure as it rolled through him.

With that initial penetration taken care of, he pulled his tentacles slickly down around Morred's cock, massaging the length and stimulating him, though the dragon barely was in his right mind. He panted heavily, flanks heaving, and tipped back, slowly pulling Morred along with him as he fell back into the water.

The rush of saltwater swelling around him drowned out all else, though there were still softer, more muted noises filtering through to the indents of his ears in the sides of his head, though they were so subtle that he barely even noticed them most of the time. He flicked his tail under the water, feeling lighter again, even though the water still exerted some pressure against him. The natural buoyancy of his body wanted to drag him back to the surface and Nerin exhaled in a stream of bubbles, though the sea dragon could hold his breath for many minutes and had no concerns at all about the abilities of his body there.

He would last, as he worked the tentacle deeper still into Morred's ass, twisting his tentacles around the dragon as his own fronds fanned out, spilling and drifting around him. The drake gasped, a bubble of used up breath escaping his lips, and Nerin reminded himself, once again, that he could not keep Morred under the water for too long. Paying attention to his partner, despite their lustful, mutual desire for one another, was and always would be of the utmost importance.

Morred looked up hazily at the sparkle of the surface above him, fractured with movements and casting rippling lines down over his green scales. He reached out, Nerin supporting his left arm with a tentacle, though he was better able to fan the fingers of his right hand through the water, marvelling briefly even at the flow of water between them, how it tickled down into the crook of each finger.

Yet he could not deny the rise of his cock, how it pulsed faintly with a rush of blood even under the water, though it was less obvious all over again just how much pre-cum was drooling from him as the ocean washed it away instantly. The length was smooth with a defined head and glands, though Nerin was quick to work a tentacle behind those glands, teasing over the sensitive flesh. He let his head roll back and from side to side, the dull pressure of the ocean bearing in against his ears.

It was simply so *good* to be back in Nerin's hold again, the sea dragon cradling him wonderfully, though some would have called him a sea monster. And perhaps Nerin had contributed to a few of the "ocean monster" myths in recent years, as he was not all that old, but he had not meant any harm with it. He was just as he was and liked his private life, even if they would not have to be so far apart from one another soon. He had plans to move to an island, having finally gained the planning permissions to build a home there. But that was just a surprise for Nerin to come to later, something that would bring the two of them even closer together than ever.

Of course, neither dragon knew that they were on the same page with their plans and surprises, both of them lining up perfectly to bring them together. But that was not about what the moment was about as Morred rocked back lightly on that penetrating tentacle, tipping down as Nerin gently guided and manipulated his body.

He slid up the underside of the sea dragon's body, nose easing over his perfectly smooth skin with nips and kisses, but he knew exactly what to do as he came face to face with Nerin's cock. If they had been better matched up in their body types, they could have been in a sixty-nine position – but Nerin's longer, more sinuous body required a few extra considerations and that was more than okay between them both. It was all about being flexible and Morred had taught Nerin a thing or two about going with the flow while Nerin taught him how to feel it out in the first place.

Morred kissed the tip of the drake's large cock, though his longer muzzle with a chunky, masculine graft to it was more than suited to taking a good length of Nerin's shaft into his mouth. He just had to be careful of his teeth, sliding his tongue out to wrap and drag down the length of that thick member, luxuriating in the moment even as his lungs pulled for air. As if reading his mind, Nerin took him back to the surface for a moment, breaking the barrier between water and air in a shatter of shimmering diamonds as the sun fractured through them. Morred sucked in a deep breath through his nostrils, focusing on that rather than the lustful aches pulsing through his body. He would need that air, even though it was unlikely Nerin would take him too deep that day. There were ways for that, but they were a little more complicated than they had the mental energy for at that time.

His ass tightened around the tentacle stretching him open, grinding back and forth as he was eased open and Nerin built up to a slow, steady thrust. It was the kind of stroke that sent a ripple through him with every push, grinding a fraction deeper every time as Morred squeezed his pucker around it, head swimming. Under the water once more, bubbles streamed faintly from his nostrils, but Morred was secure in the moment, leaning into his partner as he twined his tongue around the drake's cock and took it deep.

His jaws strained wide as he rocked his hips, though Morred could not be sure how much of his movement was his or what came from the water or his partner – but who cared about anything like that? He lapped around that cock, holding his mouth open wide, the tentacle driving up under his tail making his cock leak a drop of pre-cum every time it pushed insistently over his prostate, having thrust more than deep enough. Even in the water, he was right there in the element in that moment, experiencing it all as it was meant to be experienced. Tentacles wrapped around him and he heard Nerin moaning through the water, emboldening him to keep lapping around that cock, his tongue stretching as far down as it could, as if it was trying to get all the way to the base of it.

Nerin fared little different when it came to the lust coursing through him, like every beat of his heart sent the lure of bliss through his bloodstream, or even his nervous system. The sea dragon twisted and flowed around his partner, turning belly up so he could more easily push him back up to the surface whenever Morred needed to breathe. That meant every thirty seconds or so, so the strain on the dragon's lungs did not grow too great, but he allowed his fronds and other tentacles to spread out, giving him a greater surface area to float with.

His cock throbbed within Morred's maw and his heart sang, waves washing and lapping around his ears and head as he relaxed there, though, truly, there was very little relaxing to be done there. He shuddered as Morred's tongue scooped around him, eagerly drinking down a drop of pre-cum, and he responded by pushing his tentacle more insistently against the drake's tail hole, working it smoothly back and forth in a harder, driving rhythm. His other two tentacles, which were in active use, pulled and massaged over the drake's cock, running from base to tip in tandem and curling around his cock to drag to the end again, never quite allowing Morred to guess what sensation would come next.

There was no moment either dragon could have said was more perfect than that one, Nerin snatching a few breaths of air himself from time to time as they were both, patiently, worked up. For that interlude between them was not about the actual orgasm but the journey to it, reminding one another of the curves and nuances of each other's body, memorising every edge of the other as they had done so many times before.

Closer than ever, Nerin groaned, licking his lips, eyes blinking as water washed over them, a third eyelid, which was translucent, protecting his eyes from the salt water. He rolled back and used his tail to thrust up, pushing his cock a little deeper into Morred's maw, though he could not let need take over him too fully. Not as he concentrated on bringing his partner to the edge, using the delicate tips of his tentacles to flick over the glands as his partner grunted and groaned breathlessly under him.

He stayed there, right at the surface where Morred could more easily breathe, with a stray gull floating above, scanning the water for fish scraps it could easily pick up. Sadly, for the opportunistic seabird, it only caught a glimpse of two dragons in the throes of passion, taking from one another what would have been considered illicit, perhaps, if others saw them. Yet Nerin and Morred did not care one little bit what others thought of them – only that the two of them were safe in their love for one another, away from anyone that may ever have sought to do them harm.

One day, the world would be more accepting of the oceanic drakes and even other quadruped dragons who lived a more natural life than so-called civilised furs, but that would be as a result of all the work Morred was to do. That would come in time, but that was where the outcome was a relief and the journey arduous.

Better to take the joys where they could find them, the dragon exhaling in a rush as heat swelled in his abdomen. Morred twitched, rocking his hips forward, but the drake was helped out by a couple of tentacles pulling around his hips, supporting his thighs. He didn't even have to hold up the weight of his own body as need surged through him: a more demanding heat than he'd felt so far. Morred huffed for breath that seemed in short supply even when he wasn't in the water, tail lifting and curling up over his back while droplets of water dripped from his wings.

Yes… Yes, he was where he was meant to be, yet the route to ecstasy was not his to rush. He squeezed around the tentacle in his ass, letting out an almost needy whimper at how his body roiled with pleasure in the aftermath of that, cock twitching from the muscles at the very base of his abdomen, just above it. Oh, he needed it, but he focused on lavishing attention upon Nerin's cock, slurping and lapping along it while he let it spring wetly from his muzzle.

Nerin groaned, the sound bubbling from his lips as he laid his head back in the water, upside down, seeing the ocean beneath them, though he sensed nothing near that would cause them any trouble. He rolled his hips, tail arcing down through the water to act as a balancing weight, his heart beating harder and quicker than before. His cock throbbed openly, every pulse of pre-cum drooling from him in a wet tickle, though the long length of Morred's lapping tongue swiftly took care of that. It was even more alluring when Morred slurped along his length, his tongue practically slapping his cock in a wet splatter of pre-cum.

There was no one more salaciously lustful than Morred when the dragon was deep in the moment and that too was a thing to behold. Nerin twitched, his cock throbbing harder than ever, though he shuddered, barely even able to focus on delivering pleasure to Morred too. It was hard to focus at a time like that, although it all came naturally.

Not thinking too hard about what he was doing allowed him to exhale in a ripple of bubbles, lips barely under the surface, his body swaying and rocking with the tilt of the waves. Nearby, the boat waited for Morred and Nerin pushed away the desire to sink it, if only to keep his partner out there in the ocean with him forever.

Soon…

He wouldn't have to worry about being apart from Morred again soon, so he pressed on, letting his cock twitch within the dragon's maw as Morred engulfed his shaft once more. He rolled his hips and thrust harder without even thinking about it, his cock pounding up into Morred as his partner arched on top of him.

Morred rolled his hips back, although Nerin could see the drake was entirely focused on him. Yet he lost his senses, mildly so, as he climaxed, a suddenly rush of heat surging through his lower abdomen and exploding from his length. Long, hot jets of cum, far more powerful than they needed to be, shot into Morred's mouth, painting the inside of his maw and his tongue with thick drips of seed. The dragon clamped his mouth closed as tightly around his cock as he could, without harming Nerin with his teeth, and swallowed hard, the lewd, wet gulps cutting through even the constant wash and draw of the waves.

As Nerin lost himself in ecstasy, Morred quivered on top of him, his legs resting against the dragon as the tentacles loosened their grip on him ever so slightly – but he wasn't going anywhere in a hurry. His ass clenched hungrily around the tentacle under his tail and he tried, desperately, to buck against it, his body aching for more. Yet it was coming, that heat swirling and drawing taut within him, his cock straining on the edge with the tentacles sweeping and caressing over his cock.

They were just what he needed and he rocked his hips, letting a pulse of desire rise sharply. It was coming and he was more than ready for it. Morred groaned aloud, twisting slightly, yet he couldn't go anywhere as waves lapped around him, impaled on that tentacle and his backside shoved back towards Nerin's head. He leaned heavily on the dragon as his cock spurted, ecstasy upon him before his mind had caught up with what was happening.

It was worth it all, closer to Nerin than ever before, climaxing nearly at the same time, he licked his lips, running his tongue wetly over the dragon's cock, making sure that not a single spot was left without such a tease. His gaze fell half-lidded and he sank back a little more with an arch in his lower back, tail falling to the side with need resounding through him.

It was the kind of need that was in the process of being sated, however, his body settling down against the sea dragon as he lapped around his cock, warm and hazy with the sun on his back. Even the cool breeze no longer sent a chilling prickle along his scales as Morred relaxed there, settling back with a grind on to the tentacle while his cock spent cum into the water. It was one mess he wouldn't have to clean up, the ocean taking care of that for them, the thick spurts trailing off as a satisfied, warm glow spread through his body.

He shook his head and tried to twist around, the sea dragon sliding his tendril out of his ass so he had more range of motion. It was awkward to adjust himself on top of Nerin, but Morred more or less managed it with the drake's tentacles only lashing out a couple of times to grab him. Resting his head on the curve of Nerin's chest, the dragon grinned foolishly, giddy in the afterglow.

"Who would have ever thought I'd have a dragon of the deep for my own?" He teased, tail flicking back and forth playfully. "So… How've things been?"

Nerin laughed, his voice clearer and his throat opening with greater ease than before.

"You're so quick to recover! Can't we just…float for a while?"

"Then up in the boat for a picnic?"

"Sounds perfect."

Together, they drifted, Nerin draping his tail to steer them, so they did not drift too far. They'd need to get back to the boat soon, but, until then, they would float, relaxing and sinking into one another's bodies exactly as they needed.

The drakes had one another and that was more than enough for them.

Playing with Magic

"So… Are we going to do this or what?"

Selena grinned wickedly, the snow leopard's tail flicking back and forth as she lay stretched out along the length of the sofa. The tip of it was whiter than was typical for most snow leopards, though dark rosettes marked her fur all over, concentrating from her shoulders down to her rump. Dressed in only a lacey, blue bra and matching panties that hugged her ass, she watched her partner's eyes dart to her as if Nick simply couldn't keep his eyes off her.

Wolves are simple creatures…

And she loved him for that too, how he eyed her like he wanted to devour her, a line twitching down the side of his black-furred muzzle. The wolf was naked and she allowed herself to admire his form as he brought the book to the coffee table in the living room, the lights already turned down to a comfortable setting for an evening of delight together. The trays of finger foods they'd enjoyed while watching their favourite show (a comedy to lighten their hearts in more trying times, of course) were in the kitchen, but they wouldn't all be tidied and cleaned up until the morning.

Nick met his partner's gaze and grinned, lips parting as his dark-furred tail lifted a little, letting her get a glimpse of his muscled rump, visible even through his fur. He worked out rather a lot, though it was not merely for vanity, even if appearance was a factor there. He wouldn't have wanted to be thought a liar, of course, by saying otherwise, his sheath feeling ever so slightly tighter as his arousal grew into it.

The cat was hard to ignore, his heart skipping a beat as he eyed her rolling over on to her back and stretching luxuriously, though the wolf had to take care of the little book of fun first. He pushed the coffee table back from the sofa to give them room and swallowed as he did his best not to lose himself in the rise of her full breasts. She was built with a curvier figure that he always adored, wide hips and a full chest, though there was something about the softness of her ass that got to Nick the most.

Or maybe it was so much more than just about how they looked to one another, but the connection between them made their relationship what it was: so much more. Still, there was a part of the wolf that ached to kiss down the line of her body, straight between her breasts, and feel her quiver under him, breath quickening, as he peeled down her underwear…

Not that night, however. That night was something special, a fun time that was just for them to experience together. But a good, hot shower to wash the scent of sex and sweat from their fur afterwards, helping one another soap up, most likely would not go amiss in the.

He growled lightly in the back of his throat, no more than the faintest of rumbles, and the snow leopard shivered before him. Gods, he wanted to make her come apart under him, moaning and squirming.

"Let's get it started then, my hungry kitten."

The feline mewled and squirmed on to her belly, but her wolf was already working at the spell book. Magic, to some extent, was common in their world, with harmless things being fluid enough through most societies. Of course, every culture had a different manner of magic woven through, although they all got along well enough. Most spells could be reversed too, although furs were warned against tangling with things they didn't understand.

There were…more than a few accidents, but mostly with no serious repercussions. Those with access to more powerful spells may have had more to tangle with, but that was very much not what Nick and Selena were dealing with there. If there was one way to hone spells, even in their thin spell book, it was when furries found ways to use it for sexual purposes.

"Nostra hvon marrek testot..." He intoned softly as the cat shivered, Selena watching him intently from half-lidded eyes. "Unnest illis presta travestonus tenticalicus..."

"Oh, say it slower, baby."

Nick's lips twitched and the wolf was forced to try not to laugh, chest shaking mildly. But where was the fun in playing with one of their favourite toys without laughing a little too? Some furs could take things much too seriously, at least in his opinion.

But that was just the wolf's opinion as he set the book down, the words he'd been reciting from the pages glowing eerily. The hairs on the back of his neck prickled and his hackles tried to raise, though they were nowhere anywhere near as pronounced on an anthro as they were a feral, regardless of their position in society. His tail flicked in a smooth sweep of thick fur and Nick held his breath, a paw reaching out to clasp Selena's.

The snow leopard hung on to him as if for grounding in the moment, though her eyes were absolutely fixed on the book as the pages ruffled and fluttered back and forth. There was no semblance of a breeze or a draft in the room, but magic flickered between them, the spicy taste dancing on their tongues. Who could have known that magic, when in use, would have its own flavour?

"Yesss..."

The snow leopard hissed as the book settled down again, only to allow the pages to ripple and bulge like something was trying to work its way out from inside the book itself. She held her breath, her partner dropping to his knees beside the sofa, the swell of Nick's cock a little more obvious as his sheath pulled around it. The red tip protruded, a grey happy trail leading from his crotch to the faint indent of his belly button, and the feline switched positions to sit up on the sofa with her buttocks scooted right to the edge of the cushion.

"Nick, please!"

The wolf released her paw as he grinned widely, pink tongue flicking out salaciously against the side of his muzzle in a slow, tantalising drag. Of course, he wouldn't let his girlfriend go without, even if she simply did not have the patience in her to wait a single second more. Delicately, he pulled her underwear down her long, shapely legs with his teeth, spending a moment longer groping and squeezing her thick, powerful thighs than he had to – but just why shouldn't adore his goddess in any way possible?

Only when her underwear had slid fully from her hind paws, tossed away somewhere for them to find later, did the wolf turn his full attention to Selena, trusting his spell to run its course. His tongue lashed out against her pussy as she spread her legs wantonly for him, tracing from her perineum over her folds and to the bud of her clit – or, at least, where it was hidden. Nick did not push too quickly, lapping up with a long draw of his tongue to allow it to press into her folds and part them lightly, tasting her sweet essence where a drop of moisture already greeted his tongue.

"Mmm... You're as beautiful as ever for me, darling."

The feline gasped faintly and held on to his head, her fingers threading through the thick fur. Nick had something of a styled tuft of fur on top of his head, whereas she had long, flowing black hair, but the wolf made his natural features work for him. Her hair became trapped behind her upper back and she sofa as she wriggled, but the cat couldn't find it in herself to care as she panted and ground against him. Still, trying to get Nick to go harder than he was ready to really hadn't got her anywhere in the past, despite Selena trying the same old tricks all over again.

"Mmm, yes, please…"

Her eyes drifted over his shoulder to the book, the bulging throb rising from it slowly in a light blue hue. They came for them both, every last one of the tentacles, but neither wolf nor leopard could ever be wholly sure of where they came from. Some said magic utilised fragments from other dimensions while others said the magic itself was the energy that powered such things: it was all still very much up for debate and left to magical academics.

The sexual side was there to be enjoyed, as safely as possible, as the blue tentacles, all of varying thicknesses, bustled and churned up against one another. They crawled over Nick, being closest, and the wolf quivered, the tentacles feeling his muscles, sliding over his back and straight over his shoulders to the rounded "cannonballs" he'd been feeding in the gym.

"Oh…"

She felt the wolf's breath on her sex as he freed her clit, allowing the nub of flesh to swell more easily from its little hood, though hers was quite small and often difficult to tease out. With a deft tug of his fingers on her sex, drawing her flesh a little tauter to expose her clit, he lapped over it sensually, letting the long, slow pull of his tongue cover as much of her sex as possible.

The feline's moans drove him on, though the twitch and slither of the tentacles, even to him, was something he very much wanted to play with. He groaned in the back of his throat, eyes hazed over, but it was the kind of interlude he could sink into. It was not so much about slipping away from the rest of the world but finding something that was a little unconventional, finding a little more of himself.

Maybe that was something the wolf would have to explore more slowly, taking his time in an episode of self-reflection, but it didn't matter right then. The snow leopard groaned before him and he tipped his chin up a little so he could focus on her clit, allowing a tentacle to slide around the front of his throat and under his chin, seeking Selena's pussy.

And it was not as if Nick was going to deny the tentacles what they wanted, the spell designed to generate them – not to control what they did. That was what made playing with the tentacles as exciting as it was every time they spent an evening with them: they could never be quite sure what was going to come next, what was going to make them groan with an overload of pleasure.

The tip of one blue tentacle quested over the feline's pussy, sliding back towards her tail hole and then teasing up towards her pussy. It found what it wanted and was an easy enough girth for Selena to take as it, gently, eased inside her.

Selena moaned aloud as the tentacle stretched her out, ripples of pleasure rolling through her as her partner lapped over her clit, pausing to use his lips and swirl his tongue deliriously around the button of flesh. It would have been enough to make her lose her mind without even going into anything more, but the wolf was not one to be idle. Not as the tentacle thrust back and forth gently inside her, stretching her out and using her own natural arousal as lubrication.

It meant the tentacle had to go a little easier on her, not producing its own lubrication to take her, but every thrust worked the thickness of it a little deeper. She panted and heaved, chest rising sharply within the confines of her bra, although it was quite as if her boobs were about to spill over the top of it. Her cleavage shuddered with every snatch of air and she moaned, gripping Nick tightly, though Selena was sure she tugged too hard at his fur sometimes. The wolf never complained.

The tentacle stretched her out, thickening up with a lilt of magic, as it fucked her. Semi-translucent, a little light glanced through it as it moved, rippling and grinding with a hypnotising thrust. She panted for breath, unable to find the will to do anything more as more tentacles reached her. Even though they were already curling and twisting around Nick, taking over his thrusting motions as they wrapped around his hips and glutes, they had only just got up to the snow leopard. Selena extended one paw, palm up, allowing a tentacle to slide over her palm for her to close her fingers lightly around it, as if the two of them were old friends.

She sure felt like they were old friends when they came back to the tentacles, lusting for the filling, like they were giving up control – but in a *controlled* environment. That could well have bene key for furs like them, and others, who were so very used to keeping that control all for themselves in their daily lives, needing to manage everything. That was not a bad thing, but it was not always something sustainable for those living hard and fast, never slowing in the slightest.

That was where Nick came in, the wolf shuddering bodily as more tentacles crept around his body, some hanging around his hips and scooping down towards his cock. His hard length throbbed, fully out and ready to spend his load if the knot swelled, but the wolf could hold back for longer than that. He licked his lips, sharing his feline with the tentacles, but that was exactly what he'd set out to do.

Her skin pulled smoothly under his tongue, slickening with saliva. Yet Nick pressed on, rolling his hips lightly as tentacles, fine and delicate, twisted up and around his cock, as if they were trying to encase it. Sometimes they would open up and suck his cock down into one of them, which seemed somewhat like a living fleshlight, if he was to consider it so crudely. Panting lightly, he locked his lips around Selena's clit as the tentacles stroked up and down his cock, though they shifted and slithered in and out of one another, so he was never quite without any form of stimulation on his cock.

It was such an intense feeling it could have been over stimulating, yet Nick leaned into it with a throaty whimper that surprised even him. A tentacle teased under the root of his tail and he quivered, almost freezing in place, but he could not forget Selena. With the snow leopard shivering before him, rocking and grinding her hips into his snout, she gave him something special to focus on.

With the taste of her arousal clinging to his lips and mouth, the wolf sucked on her clit, tongue flitting up against it. Yet the tentacles rubbed over his member, some of the thinner ones even dipping into his sheath, teasing sensitive nerve endings that never usually were given such attention.

Even the living room around them seemed to fall away, like he and the snow leopard existed with one another alone – and the tentacles. Nick groaned against her as she gasped and the tentacle seemed to pulse where it was rammed into her stretched sex, but the wolf didn't ease off. A moderately-sized tentacle tested his resistance by pressing at his tail hole and he exhaled in a rush of warm breath over Selena's pussy, but he relaxed around it as much as he could, allowing it entrance.

However, it was not easy for him to take anal stimulation, even as the tentacle thinned out and worked into him, the magic adjusting to the needs of his body. His tail lifted obligingly and he lost himself a little more, the cat before him moaning and gripping his head more tightly than ever.

Selena gasped, thrusting her hips forward, but the cat was already lost to lust. Her pussy dripped with her arousal, the tentacle thrusting into her with a lewd, wet squelch, though her body opened up beautifully around it. Panting heavily, she twisted, rolling her head from one side to the other, yet there was nothing Selena wanted to do in the slightest to stop the rising heave of arousal swelling through her.

No... It was the snow leopard's to take as she delighted in eyeing up her partner, watching how his ears twitched, like they wanted to go all the way back. It was obvious from the push of his body that the tentacles were grinding teasingly up into his ass and she smirked inwardly at the notion that the wolf was getting what he wanted again. Maybe one day they would get around to trying out a bit of pegging, but the muscled, black wolf had always been sensitive to such things.

The tentacle thrust harder inside her, a fat length that really didn't look at all like it should have fit inside her, letting her pussy strain around it as she relished in the moment. The magic lifted her up, the blue tentacles snaking around her and toying with her bra, but, between them and the wolf, there was nothing else for Selena.

Lust billowed inside her and she gave a feline-like yowl as desire coursed through her, orgasm taking her at last. Oh, how she needed it, hips rocking weakly up to Nick's touch, though she could barely put an arch into her lower back as she humped and ground. Her tongue slipped out in a pink pull. Waves of ecstasy rolled through her, though they all seemed to come in time with the lap of the wolf's tongue and the thrust of the tentacle, as if all three of them were perfectly in sync with one another.

Maybe it was so and maybe it was not, but it didn't matter. Not if pleasure was at the forefront of their minds, her pussy soaked as the tentacle gleamed with an overload of her arousal. It dripped to the sofa, to be cleaned up later, and the tentacle snapped her bra from her, pulling it sharply back from her shoulders. Somehow, she was dimly aware of her paw leaving Nick's head, only to be wrapped up in the tentacles and wrenched demandingly up over her head.

Oh, now things are getting interesting!

The snow leopard mewled as more and more tentacles poured from the book, encasing both of them in a twist and swathe of blue. Wrenching the pair from the sofa and the carpet, the tentacles took all they wanted from the two of them, the wolf's arms yanked behind his back and bound while his legs were spread for the pounding of a tentacle stretching out his tail hole.

He grunted, but a tentacle wound up into his mouth, sliding past his gasping lips, to silence him. Not that the wolf minded as he relished in the undercurrent of submission, what was so very difficult for him to acknowledge most of the time. Tipping forward, the wolf was barely even aware of his orientation as sensation overwhelmed him. Besides the mass of tentacles, which seemed numerous enough to fill the entire living room, he could only see the snow leopard, hanging upright with her arms up above her head.

Nick moaned, the tentacle pounding his tail hole more alluring than ever, his body quaking around it. Strangely for him, it was more difficult for him to orgasm from anal penetration alone – but maybe that was why the magic of the tentacles curled around his cock, pleasuring him in other ways first. He could never be quite sure whether the magic remembered previous encounters or if he was applying more meaning to them than there could be.

It didn't matter, not as he relaxed, sucking on the tentacle in his mouth, though he struggled to work his tongue around it, with how it thrust back and forth. It could have been simulating a cock grinding into his mouth, something he had not yet experienced, but he would only have that with the tentacles and the snow leopardess who was the complete and utter love of his life.

Selena heaved for breath, though there barely even seemed to be a break between one orgasm and the flow of pleasure. Two tentacles with small "mouths" wetly locked on to her nipples, sucking with such delicious force that the feline could not help squirming and squealing with delight. How could she not, after all, when such pleasure coursed through her? Electric tingled lanced out from her nipples as the erogenous zones were teased, her pussy squeezing around the tentacle still spreading her open.

As if to join Nick in similar sensations, another slightly smaller tentacle (from the first that had slid into her pussy before it had grown) probed at her tail hole and she tried her best to keep her flicking, feline tail out of the way. That was harder than ever as lust pulled through her, baring her teeth in a feral grin that suited her as a feline, the low light gleaming on her teeth as they were exposed. Yet there was no manner of threat there, only desire, the tentacles sliding over her thighs and squeezing around her nipples, dizzying her senses.

That was not enough to stop the tentacles, however, as she fell deeper and deeper into debauchery. They curled up and around her neck as if to mimic a collar, though she let her gaze roam hungrily over the wolf, sharing the experience with her partner still. They may not have been in contact with each other still, but the connection between them sizzled as Nick let out grunting groans and muffled whines around the tentacle filling his mouth.

"Ah… Just…give in…to them…" Selena moaned as loudly as she could, though it was hard to see past the haze of her own pleasure even when she wanted to help out Nick too. "You want it… Let them!"

She cried out with a thrust of her hips, tentacles stuffing both her pussy and her tail hole full, grinding up against one another through the thin barrier that separated her two entrances from one another. Nick quivered, eyes flicking up to her with a watery sheen, and she smiled encouragingly to him, her body quivering as the tentacles pulled her legs apart even further than before.

"Mmmmm…"

Selena groaned, relaxing a little more, though her body felt like it was providing a tighter fit than ever to the tentacles. They pumped up inside her and she strained pleasurably against her bonds, feeling the tight pull and restriction around her wrists, letting her tail hole be spread wider and wider.

But not too wide, of course. It was all about sensuality and pleasure: not going past the point where it would have been such to her. The same would be true for Nick and Selena was more certain than ever that he'd reach his high more explosively than ever. She couldn't *wait* to see cum jetting from his cock in a pure arc, spraying from him as if his body simply could not hold it back for a single moment more.

The wolf squirmed, huffing and panting, but Nick could not pretend at any kind of control for a single moment longer. It was not for him as he released his grip on that imagined control just a little more, letting it slide through his fingers like it was hardly settling there.

It was much too much, the pull of tentacles wrapping around his thighs, keeping his legs lewdly spread, and the pound of the one speeding up in his ass making his head spin. Yet the bondage kept him in position and he relished in that too, his guts churning with longing.

He needed…*more*. Even when it was too much, perhaps he needed more too. It didn't make sense and, still, it didn't have to make sense, not as his cock drooled pre-cum, dripping over all the tentacles over-stimulating his cock in rolling, sinuous strokes. He couldn't even see any of his cock other than the red tip, his sheath feeling full as more tentacles still squirmed and twisted about within.

They found his balls too, curling around them and sliding back and forth, the magic clearly taking note of what made Nick squirm and jolt the most readily. Yet it was merely the feel of having them held, only very lightly squeezed, that did it for Nick. The wolf thrashed and twisted, gasping for breath.

It would not ease the tightness in his chest, however, as he rolled his hips, shamelessly thrusting into the tentacles. His cat grinned at him and he took solace in that, knowing there was no harm to come to him there. Nick could lose himself in sensation, the tentacle in his mouth tasting faintly of raspberries, powering smoothly over his tongue, the raw force of it forcing his tongue down into the bottom of his mouth between the lines of his teeth.

It was not needed. Frankly, the wolf didn't need to do anything at all, not as the tentacles pleased him, rocking his body with every stroke. His tail lifted and the tentacles eagerly snatched it up, wrenching it high so it wouldn't get in the way. Nick had no intention at all of pulling it down, however, as he licked at the tentacle in his mouth as much as he was able. He was there to be used, need rising within him, his entire body prickling with heat.

Yet the wolf's eyes were fixed on his lover as the snow leopardess bucked and moaned in turn, letting pleasure roll through her. He couldn't look at anything else, not even with so many twisting, writhing lengths trying to dominate his range of vision. He could be lost in that moment and found again later, the tentacle driving and pounding up into his welcoming hole deeper than before. It ground over his prostate and he let out a broken howl around the stuffing in his maw, trying to close his lips around it fully but only finding himself drooling instead.

But he would not and could not hold back as the tentacles fucked him to bliss, his cock throbbing in their hold. The muscles in his lower abdomen tensed, but he could not even see his cock twitch, the rush of climax roaring in his ears. Nick climaxed with a broken howl, there for every single moment as desire pulsed through him, carrying his body onward as he shot his load. His cock throbbed with every spurt of cum as his body gave up all it had to hold, eyes closed, losing himself.

The feline watched him intently, but the strain of two tentacles fucking her at once was far too much. Oh, how she wished she was pressed up against the wolf in that moment, able to fully share in the experience with him, but maybe that would come next time. She strained towards him, her chest bowing out as she did her best to get to him, but she could take it all as she wanted, watching his hips judder, pushing forward even as the tentacle crammed into his ass throbbed and pulsed, stretching him wider than she was sure he'd ever been before.

That wolf has a lot to experience…

It was the snow leopard's time, however, to exult in the moment as she groaned, Selena's head falling back as the warming heat within her built and built. She tried to hold on, wanting to be there in the moment for as long as possible, but there was nothing truly she could do against the lustful "wrath" of the tentacles. They slammed into her as if they were trying to bore all the way through her body – and yet they never quite pushed too far, her entire body strained and teetering right on the brink of her boundaries being stretched to their limit.

And then she cried out, losing control as the tentacles enveloped her, wrapping all the way around her body in a heaving mass at the point of climax. It roared through her and she tried to hang on as much as she could, huffing and panting, her chest rising and heaving too sharply as her blood ran hot. Once again, her arousal soaked the tentacle in her sweet essence, her tail hole clenching with such force that she almost stalled the tentacle in thrusting. That was, however, only for a moment as it ground tenaciously deeper, the tip softening as it squashed up against her cervix.

She didn't hold back as lust snarled within her, though her lips parted in a soundless cry as orgasm snatched her up. The snow leopard allowed it to course through her, throb after throb, peaks dragging her higher and the troughs barely even letting her go for a breath of relief. Not that Selena needed or wanted it in the slightest, ravenous for more, the tentacles parting like a curtain to let her see her wolf once more, panting and heaving in the aftermath of climax.

Ecstasy claimed her and she closed her eyes, hips rocking and jerking of their own accord. There was no control she could have possibly claimed to have over herself as she soaked the tentacle in her wetness, the length of it gleaming with every drop she had to give. Yet even the best of orgasms had to come down sooner or later, softening to bring her back to reality and a sultry slither of blue lengths around her, one of them probing curiously at her lips.

"Ah…" She panted, Selena parting her lips to take a tentacle softly against them in a wet, lewd kiss. "So, you're not done with us yet?"

Of course, the magic would last longer and the two of them rocked and moaned in the hold of the tentacles, letting bliss come to them, over and over again. Until they both met in the centre of the living room once more, the coffee table knocked over, pushed into one another's arms for a deeply lustful, salacious kiss.

In the kiss, they shared their passion, Nick kissing the snow leopard harder than ever, an edge of desperation to his embrace. Yet they were both exactly where they longed to be, panting and grunting, waiting for what the tentacles had in store for them next.

Playing with magic, whether one anticipated what was coming or not, certainly opened up some new doors in their relationship! And only time would tell just how far Nick and Selena would go…

The Spell

Jordan licked his lips, the zebra's ropey tail flicking back and forth as he pawed through the spell book. It was something he'd used before but never for such lewd, self-serving needs — but where could the harm really be? His black and white mane had been dyed pink and blue, with some white left in it naturally, to show off who he was, though his legs parted, naked from head to hoof, exposing the soft folds of a pussy there. His stud-pussy.

That was a good way to look at it and the zebra turned off the TV with a lazy push of the remote control, tapping in the spell code (hey, things had updated over the years). It would do the trick for him as his tail flicked over the edge of the sofa and he sat up. Need tingled through him, his bare chest showing the light scars, which were only more obvious because of the lighter, thinner coat of hair he bore. Zebras most certainly were not known for being fluffy or anything of that ilk.

The living room was sparsely furnished, but everything Jordan picked up, whether it was new or second hand, was, of course, excellent quality. The zebra loved a bargain, but he loved belongings that lasted well and looked the part even more. That was why he'd been able to splurge on the magical additions to his phone app system, though magic didn't seem to be used for anything grand anymore.

Mostly just for perverts, he thought with a grin, grey lips stretching as need pulled at the pit of his belly. Perverts would keep anything alive and lead to the most developments in technology, he was quite sure. After all, what else could be needed there, other than something to lift the mind and soul, a little bit of delight?

The spell activated with a chime and he grinned, waiting for the magic to take hold. It always took a second for the spell to come through, though it wasn't directly through his phone. It was deeper than that, magic innate with the fabric of the world, but it always came with a price. Monetary, of course, but that didn't bother him much when it was something he wanted.

He spread his legs as the tentacles emerged, sucking and pulling out from underneath the sofa, slithering over the wooden floorboards as if they had always been there. The zebra grunted and pushed his legs apart further, the muscle in his thighs bulging as he leaned back and put his hands behind his head.

"Oh, fuck yeah..."

He blinked at the tentacles slithering up over the edge of the sofa, crawling towards him with single-minded intent. That was, after all, all they were created for, the sort of thing that would not exist if not for him pulling at the spell, using what someone else had created to wind together those threads of reality again.

For it was Jordan's moment and his alone to take as he pleased, leaning back and settling there as he exposed his sex for the tentacles. They twisted and writhed, though did not bind his legs, merely pushing at his big hooves to widen the space between his thighs even further. Obligingly, the zebra scooted his firm glutes even closer to the edge of the sofa, so the tentacles had easier access to him, probing lightly at his dampening sex.

The folds of his stud-pussy were plump and full, the sort of sex he didn't want to hide in the slightest. In fact, he was rather proud of it and gently adjusted his position to pull at the top of his stud-pussy, exposing his clit a little more. The thick swell of it protruded from its hood and he grunted, the tentacles taking the chance to slither between his folds, gently parting them.

"Ah – fuck!"

Jordan moaned and rolled his hips, letting it all happen, tangible desire inside him aching to be released. It was not abstract, for he felt it swelling through him, the pounding pulse of it aching deep in his chest. The tentacles knew that too as they pressed against his sex, gently rubbing back and forth so the tip of one particular tendril was coated in his slick arousal.

"Mmm… Yes, yes… Just like that…"

Jordan could have muttered his desires aloud or not: it really didn't matter to the tentacles. He licked his lips hungrily, his broad, fleshy tongue sweeping out and between his lips, from left to right. In the moment, he sank into it, the curtains drawn but still allowing a crack of evening light through from the streetlights outside. The living room was dim now that the TV was off with only a single side lamp left on for illumination, but Jordan didn't need more than that.

The tentacle pushed insistently into his stud-pussy, stretching him out nicely around a thick filling. Instinctively, the zebra bucked his hips, rolling them forward and sliding further down against the back seat cushions of the sofa. He wouldn't have said he was comfortable there, but he was still where he needed to be, where he wanted to be, a deep-seated hunger for pleasure roiling in his belly.

More tentacles pulled up his body, eagerly exploring his abdominal muscles and sliding insistently over his pectorals, taking care of every inch of his form. A gruff snort broke from him as they drew over his shoulders, thickly rounded out with muscle, and it was all the zebra could do not to flex for them, not to indulge in a moment of vanity right where he could – and no one would know.

Jordan squeezed his stud-pussy around the tentacle, experimenting with it and tightening his muscles over and over again, just to see what felt good. His tail flicked back and forth in a ropey "thwap" against the sofa, but the zebra barely even heard it. He was too caught up in grinding his hips forward at the tentacle, exposing the tighter pucker of his tail hole so it may grind into him there too.

Why not indulge? There was no reason not to except perhaps thinking he did not deserve that bliss, those highs of pleasure that were for him to take in that moment alone. Grunting, his chest rose sharply for a snatch of air, though one of the zebra's hands gripped the seat of the sofa, trying to root himself in the moment as pleasure threatened to overwhelm him.

"Yes… Mmph."

The tentacle drove up into his stud-pussy, grinding passionately back and forth with thrust after thrust, his sex swiftly wetting around it. It was hard for him not to be turned on and that was one way in which he was glad his body was as it was; it made it an awful lot easier for him to be aroused without anyone else catching on. It would have been difficult to hide a throbbing erection, after all, and Jordan grinned, rocking his hips forward as the tentacle thrust deeply into him.

It was simply exquisite, all in the best of ways, his head spinning mildly. He pressed his hooves into the carpet, bearing down and spreading them as his thighs trembled, the vibration rolling down into his calves. The tentacle teasing over his ass ground back and forth, stimulating sensitive nerve endings as he moaned and flicked his tail. There was nothing else for him to do but relax into it as the tentacle slowly spread his hole and pushed inside.

"Ah!"

He was barely in control as he laid back, huffing and panting through darkly flared nostrils. Desire coursed through him and it was all Jordan could do not to sink his teeth into his lip until it bled, but that would not have made the moment any better for him. Blood was not often all that alluring to a prey species, after all. Still, the zebra grunted throatily and shook his head, his dyed mane brushing back against the bed.

His body tightened around the tentacles pounding his holes, grinding and thrusting, every stroke sending him deeper and deeper into pleasure. As the tentacles pulled around the sofa, they closed around his legs, nearly pulling him off the edge of it, but he was still where he needed to be. He blinked hazily, throbbing need pulsing through him – but that was for Jordan to take as the strain in both his holes pulsed desperately through him.

And the zebra didn't hold back in the slightest as orgasm crashed over him, pouring over him as he was being drowned in it – but it was the kind of wave he could ride out. He gasped and chuffed throatily as a hoof kicked out, almost losing his footing where he'd braced with both hooves, his stud-pussy squeezing and pulling erratically around the tentacle. He needed more, so much more, but the tentacles sped up even through his climax, slamming into him as, abruptly, bulges rippled and surged demandingly down their lengths.

Panting heavily, heated waves of prickling bliss coursing through him, the zebra watched as the bulges reached his body, squeezing up inside him and stretching him wider still – if only for a moment. Yet there was nothing to stop them as he twisted and half sat up, his body suddenly trembling with the need to contain a new pleasure.

Thick loads of cum exploded within his holes, an overdose of seed that bloated out his belly in only a few throbbing spurts of it. Jordan kicked out and found himself sliding to the floor, glad that the coffee table allowed him at least enough room to move, a hand on his abdomen as it swelled and bloated out. His skin stretched around the intrusion of so much seed, though not a single drop leaked from him either, the tentacles seemingly keeping it all trapped inside him.

"Ah… Ah, fuck…"

Jordan moaned, head back on the sofa while his legs remained spread, clasped tightly around the thighs by the tentacles. The squashy bloat of his belly ached through him and still the zebra wantonly pressed both hands into it, indenting his flesh, fingers digging greedily in. Yet the sensation that he was being overfilled swelled through him, like his body was simply not going to hold it all – but he had to! For Jordan simply had no choice in the matter as his womb stretched to accommodate and his guts bubbled faintly with all the tentacles pumped into him.

Out and out and out… His stomach swelled past the size of a football to a beach ball and then right out to an exercise ball, his skin growing firmer all the time as if his body was reaching its limit. Yet magic had a pull to it too and his body was more than able to handle it – as long as he was running the app with the spell, of course. But that had never been a problem before and, frankly, he didn't expect it to be a problem.

He could languish there, both hands resting on his sloshing, gurgling stomach as his body bloated, finally full with all the tentacles had to offer. Left there, leaning back with too much extra weight on his body to even think about staggering upright once more.

"Unff… Yes…"

The aftershocks of orgasm coursed through him, fading gently, his stud-pussy slick around the tentacle slipping from him, his holes left gaping and yet still holding all the seed inside. Maybe it was its rightful place, but his head was too hazy to follow the devious thought far. Jordan would think about that later, but there would not be anything to worry him there, for his body would absorb it all, his stomach naturally deflating, in a few hours. Until them, he tried to reach around the swell of his belly to his sex in a way he'd never had to before, grunting and puffing while his fingers ghosted over the swollen, sensitive button of his clit.

With need trembling a hair's breadth under the surface and the app having concluded its session for him with the tentacles, Jordan settled down with a smile pulling lightly at his lips, pleasure and only pleasure at the forefront of his mind. What else could the trans zebra, after all, consider when he was weighed in place just like that with a heavy womb full of seed?

One little spell, after all, could give a lot of fun...

Out in the Water

The otter dived through the waves, caring not for what may have been below the surface in the tropics, exhilaration coursing through her. What trouble did Atamai think she'd have from sharks and the like when she was out in the water as she was, one of the predators – if not of the deep? Sea snakes, however, may have been more of a problem to all.

The warm waters of the Pacific, close to Tahiti, were mostly safe for her, for she knew how to navigate the currents, though Atamai had grown up, of course, on the mainland, like most. The islands were difficult to live on those days, with locals being often pushed out in favour of tourists – or the standard of living would have been vastly different from what she was used to. However, for her holiday out there, the sea otter had needed to take on a "working holiday" of sorts, but she was more than happy to do that so she could experience the world and the oceans like that.

However, she would always turn back to the water, regardless of where her work and travels on land took her, surfacing in a spray of saltwater, her black hair, cut short above her shoulders, clinging to her body like it had abruptly lost any sense of substance it may have had. The greenery of a nearby island beckoned and she lazily eyed it, cataloguing her location and thinking nothing more of it. She could swim back to shore anytime she liked: for the moment, she was busy enjoying the swell, how the waves beckoned her to play with them.

However, there was someone else out there in the water with her and Atamai had no intention of leaving them out there alone, untended to. The otter grinned and plunged back below the surface into the quiet world of the ocean, for her hearing was not sensitive enough to truly enjoy the cacophony of soft sounds down there.

She swam fluidly, her whole body working as one to pump her way through the water. It was different for an otter to swim rather than a shark anthro, for they had their tails to power them through the water with a side-to-side pumping motion. She was suppler, her tail guiding and directing her in the water, helping her make quicker turns, rather than powering her through the ocean. Her arms laid back to her sides or led the way to carve through the water before her if she stretched them up over her head. Either way, the otter was one with the ocean and languished there, desire coursing through her.

She wanted to be one, truly...but she could not. But maybe that was a good thing too, for she was not restricted to the water either.

Atamai dove to the coral reef below, though the water there was not too deep for her as she tempted at swimming in a little closer to shore. A black tip reef sharp investigated her but swiftly turned away the moment she faced him head-on. They were not brave sharks, even if they were often swimming in larger groups, often the cause of bites amongst tourists for furs didn't always treat them with the same respect they should other sharks.

He wouldn't bother her and she swam further, turning on her side to scan the area. The blue water was exceptionally clear that day and she saw further than most furs would, but her kind and other ocean-faring anthros could often boast a benefit in the water, which made sense. A Stellate puffer fish, with the knobbly, rougher sort of balloon-like body, scooted along while a shoal of butterfly fish swam together, moving as one form. She smiled at them, watching them go, though there were many more fish down there too, if she wanted to catch something more suitable for cooking later on. In terms of watching, however, she was rather partial to the blue hue of the parrotfish down there.

Where are you?

Yet she was looking for someone, or something special. They were there, waiting for her, and she sculled through the water, floating above the reef. It was a vulnerable spot and she kept an eye out for reef sharks and silkies, even though she was sure they would see her as one of their own. Sea otters, even anthros, were simply not their natural prey and she only had to not aggravate them – or rile them up into making an investigatory bite.

The reef was quieter that day after the initial blacktip reef shark and she swam deeper, into a rocky formation where her friend usually resided. She could not have said whether they were a he or a she or an it – but it was more likely that such a twisting beastie had no gender at all. When they were what they were, they didn't need it.

They were to be found tucked into rocks and crevices, a writhing mass of sultry tentacles without any suckers, and Atamai's lips twitched in a smile as she popped back up to the surface for a full breath of air. Only then did she dive down, the water pressing lightly in on her ears as she exhaled, a stream of bubbles flitting from her lips and nostrils.

Hello, sweetheart.

Warmth poured through the otter as she swam down to the purple-pink tentacle waving gently at her from the rocks. They had secured themselves away in a different spot that day, which was why it had taken her so long to track them down, but they had never meant to hide from her. They simply moved through the ocean when there were not prying eyes on them. She'd never seen them fully out from their hiding spots, but that was up to them and Atamai was not going to force them to do anything they were not comfortable with.

No… That had happened to her a long time ago, but she had changed. For Atamai had not always been the otter she was, her pink bikini hiding the light scarring where her breasts sat, though it was softly hidden by her fur most of the time too. On the lower half, it had not been any question at all to her as to whether or not she wanted to go for bottom surgery, being assigned male at birth – but the advancements in medicine had given her the shape on the outside that fit exactly who the otter was on the inside.

So, being transgender, she understood from another perspective how it may have felt for the tentacle monster of the ocean to be drawn into the light. Her life experience may not have been theirs, or exactly that of any other anthro, but it offered her a more sympathetic perspective. Maybe they were not ready yet for anyone to see them? Either way, the otter would let them have her any way they pleased, treating them as the equal, absolutely, they were.

Atamai flicked her tail, following the tentacle that swayed back and forth as if it was nothing more than a frond of kelp. The otter reached for the tentacle, which wound gratefully between her hands and around her arms, though it was not trying to bind her in the slightest. It merely played with her body, flitting along her forearms in a feather-light touch that ghosted along her soft fur.

Her tail flicked under the water and she exhaled a little, more bubble streaming from her lips. Yet the otter had not a lick of fear in her for the tentacle monster she courted. Others would have thought her insane for swimming out as far from shore without a safety net – let alone playing with strange tentacles out in the ocean. So, why shouldn't the otter flirt with danger, even if, for her, it was merely imagined.

Oh, I miss you when you slither away…

Of course, the otter could not vocalise her appreciation of the tentacle monster of the waters without swimming in a flurry of bubbles back to the surface – and she didn't want to, not now she was down there. Her monster would have to remain tucked into its nook, although Atamai was quietly confident she could judge just how far those tentacles would extend, allowing her to push back to the surface. Unfortunately for Atamai, she could only hold her breath for around seven-and-a-half minutes, although the tentacle beastie had never been against helping her back up for a breath of air before.

Her skin prickled and tingled erotically as she sank into the flow of water around her, enjoying how it caressed her fur. Her tail swung lightly, helping her stay upright in the water, her centre of gravity just right for balancing the otter against the pull of the current.

Yet she had to dart back to the surface for a breath of air – and those pink-purple tentacles followed her. Atamai looked down as she swam, the pressure of the water sweeping over her head and neck, but it was worth it to catch a glimpse of how the shimmering fractures of the surface danced over the tentacles, forever patterning them and the rest of the ocean floor with an ever-changing mark. Her eyes instinctively wanted to follow it, once again revelling in the majesty of the ocean, how she felt most at home in it.

"Ah!"

She gulped fresh air, black hair once again slick to her face, but her chest heaved, taking in all she could. She had to hold on to what she yearned for, even as the tentacles crept up around her thighs, risking discovering as they snaked out so very far from their hiding place, but she hoped she would be able to keep an eye on their surroundings.

For there was one thing the otter knew intimately and that was exactly what the tentacles wanted from her, from her body, each and every time she sought them out. With her lungs full of air, once again, she allowed the tentacles to add more weight to her legs, bringing her down into the midpoint between the surface and the sand. Below, the sand was marked with faint, waving lines that showed the passage of both the water over it and smaller sea creatures, though the latter tended to leave more distinct tracks that cut through that softness of the pattern.

There was little time for her to relish in her environment, however, as she parted her lips, enjoying the salty flow of the ocean over her tongue. The tentacles wound around and around her legs, gently grasping her, though Atamai was sure she could have wriggled free if needed.

Not that the otter wanted that in the slightest, however, not as the tentacles quested up her thighs and between her legs, teasing lightly over her sensitive inner thighs. They played at the edge of her bikini bottoms and the otter tipped her head back, doing her best to relax into the hold of tentacles, even as her body wanted to thrust and grind, to take all she craved right then and there.

Please… Take me…

They both needed something from each other, after all, even though the otter knew there was more to the tentacle monster than just that. She only wished she could coax them out a little more, getting to know them on a more intimate, personal level still, but the tentacles had to be respected too. Maybe, in time, she'd come to see what may be had between them.

Atamai moaned as they pulled at her bikini bottoms, tugging at them gently. They could have just slithered against the folds of her sex, the small scars nicely hidden by her fur a little higher up, even if the fur was somewhat uneven over them. It didn't matter to her, not as her body matched who she was, and she groaned, bubbles streaming from her lips, as the tip of one tentacle, rounded and soft, teased over her tight entrance. She would have liked to be a little looser, naturally, than she was, not needing to be worked up as slowly as was the case, but that was most certainly something Atamai could work with.

She was as she was and the otter rolled her hips forward as she settled there, her bikini bottoms slowly peeled down. Thankfully for her, all but one time, the tentacle beastie had returned them to her all but one single time, but they had swiftly learned, which was one more thing that led her to believe there was more to the tentacles than they had, so far, let out.

Atamai's chest hitched and she rocked her hips lightly, though the tentacles pushed her back to the surface for another breath, waves lapping over her head. The otter twisted faintly, too interested in the soft squash of the tentacles pushing over her pussy, very gently parting her folds. They were tucked in close to her body, small and neat, but the tentacles knew exactly how to handle the otter: they'd spent more than enough time together, after all.

They rubbed back and forth along her folds, allowing her to push against them at her own pace, though there was still a sensitive spot with her clit. It was broader and flatter and best stimulated by grinding over it, the otter's head trying to loll back as warmth spread through her.

Oh, it was as exquisite as ever, but Atamai wanted more, so much more, as the tentacles crawled up her body, grazing her hips and winding around her waist. They would bind her more tightly when the time was right, but they had to get into position first, as if they were tenderly adoring her with every brush and tease, sliding over her shoulders and wrapping around her biceps. She grunted in the back of her throat, another bubble bursting from her lips, her chest already feeling a little tight from being under the water for so long.

She had to breathe, but she ignored that need, trusting her needs entirely over to the tentacle monster. No more than that, of course, was needed as she moaned and let waves of soft desire course through her, seemingly fuelled with every beat of her heart, sending blood around her body. Lust tracked through the network of her veins and she stretched out her fingers as her right wrist as tightly gripped, a small tentacle pushing at her pussy.

Yes! Please!

Atamai pushed with her hips, demanding more, and the tentacles were more than willing to satisfy every last little bit of her need. They took it gently, however, using the smooth, rounded tip of the tentacle to slide into her cunny, but, of course, having sex underwater came with the added challenge of any slickness around her sex being swiftly washed away, if she had tried to use any lube before heading out there. That was why they had to be patient about things, the tentacle working its way back and forth, applying a little more pressure with every tease to slide a little deeper into her with every push.

The otter barely even felt the resistance, too caught up in the moment as she floated there, the tentacles lovingly wrapped around her, desire flowing. She was right where she needed to be, eyes barely open – and to think she could have at all kept an eye on their surroundings was a jest indeed. Her pussy tightened around the tentacle, giving an experimental squeeze, and she tried to ripple around it, though Atamai doubted she'd ever have intense control over the muscles down there. Her clenches were light at best, but she still trembled every time she tried it out.

It was all worth it, everything, so very much. She groaned, lips parted, sucking in a gulp of air as she was raised to the surface, trusting even her ability to breathe to the tentacles. They would look after her, she was sure, and she had to put her faith in them if she hoped they would, eventually, allow the same in reciprocation one day.

Maybe. There was no pressure there.

The tentacle teasing up inside her pussy thrust back and forth, a good girth for her to bear down on, though her body sang with every stroke, wanting more. She would take more too, if she got to hang out in the ocean for longer, but that would depend entirely on what the two of them wanted. It reached her innermost barrier but did not push harder against it, always knowing exactly how deep it could go without pushing limits too far.

And she loved that, having even the boundaries of her body respected. The tentacles were not about ego or anything like that, just about pleasure and the experience of life itself. Blinking her eyes open, she locked her gaze on to the tentacle between her thighs, which thickened up as her pussy was taken, grinding back and forth in rougher strokes that felt like she, in a way, was being claimed. Atamai would have liked to say she'd made a "claim" on the tentacles too, but perhaps that too was something that would have to come in good time.

She was there for the moment, however, hanging suspended in the grasp of the tentacles, her back arched beautifully. It was as if she was prey that they'd caught – and yet she could never be such when she was the one too who'd hunted down the tentacles. Her tail hung beneath her as her body was teased, lusciously caressed as the tentacles slid under the back of her bikini top and wormed their way down the front, curling around her breasts without removing the bikini from her. That might have made their task easier, but sometimes that dexterity was not in their heart.

It was as if they were in something of a rush, a desperate fervour trembling through every thrust of the tentacle up into her as another ground firmly over her clit, sending a jolt of lust through her. Yes… Yes, she needed it and they wanted it too, letting the otter groan and rock deliriously within their hold. There was nothing else for Atamai in a moment like that, her hips rocking, squeezing as hard as she could and yet knowing that she was there for the pleasure of the tentacles, letting them use her body in the very best way possible.

Nothing else mattered or ever could matter as she let her body roll and twist lightly with the push of the water around her, the teasing twists of the tentacles. Her body ached for orgasm and yet she needed more than that still and would have been panting if she had been above the surface. The tightness in her chest burned faintly and she inhaled gratefully as her face once again broke the surface, white sea foam clinging to her fur and whiskers for a moment before it dripped away.

Down under the water again, away from the course of the waves lapping over and into one another, she could lose herself again in her own little world, a world where she could slip away from it all. The tentacles twisted around her breasts, holding them tightly, and she groaned from the stimulating massage, how her body felt like it was on fire even with the cooler ocean around her.

Her body, however, needed it, despite everything. She grunted and clenched a paw into a fist, but she couldn't do anything to hasten her pleasure. Just when she felt like she was growing close to orgasm, the tentacles slowed, thrusting more slowly, more patiently, and letting her settle deeper into the moment. But Atamai was not there to have any sense of control over herself, still finding it unusual how frustration and desire could build just like that at the same time.

She hissed lightly, clenching her jaw – but she didn't want to bring tension into her body like that. Not as her glutes squeezed and muscles the otter so very rarely had to think about came into play; she just felt everything moving smoothly together as she swam, more often than not. Her lower back pulled as she arched and she felt the stretch straining through her entire body, shoulder blades driving back as the tentacles helped draw her seamlessly into position.

Atamai's hair floated around her face, a little sweeping briefly across her eyes, but the otter could not pause to sweep it away. She was lost there, luxuriating in it, her lips parted as a tentacle probed at them ad she gladly accepted it between her lips. Her hips pumped and the otter swung her tail through the water, need rising with a fierce, fiery snap within her that was completely out of keeping with the water cooling her down. It was as if her body was, abruptly, out of sync with the world around her, made to dance by the pounding, trembling beat of the tentacles, how they gripped her and brought her right to the edge.

That time, however, they did not slow in the slightest, allowing the otter to revel in every sordid second of her sex squeezing around them, the tight filling feeling, all of a sudden, like it was going to be too much for Atamai. But it was most certainly not too much, not in the slightest, not as she groaned and the tentacles rolled her forward in the water, so she was tipped at an angle with her chest facing down, though still with her head at the highest point.

Ecstasy surged through her, orgasm an intense pulse that commanded every last scrap of her attention. Atamai moaned, bubbles streaming with the sound from her lips, yet even the otter could not be sure how much of it was heard beneath the surface.

She didn't care. Not as she exulted in bliss searing through her, her body rocking with desire. Her sex squeezed passionately down the length of the tentacle tenderly stretching her pussy, although the otter didn't control that. The tentacle thrust, seeming larger than before – but maybe it was the otter who was tighter than before, her entire body contracting with raw desire around the pink tentacle, wanting it to give her all it was willing to share.

With the pressure around her breasts, tentacles encircling and compressing tenderly, she floated there. Lust held her where she needed to be and Atamai floated, only aware that she had been brought back to the surface when cooler air licked over muzzle and she inhaled deeply, instinctively snatching at air. Alas, her orgasm eased down too quickly, her body left warm and exhilarated, blinking underwater as she sank into the world she adored, a writhing mass of pink and purple tentacles flowing around her like a kelp forest.

Laughing, the otter relaxed into them, although they did not slide from her pussy, instead keeping her comfortably stretched open around them. The strain was perfect, her body comfortably full, though the hunger inside her was not to be satisfied so quickly.

With a questing rock of her hips, she asked without words if the tentacles wanted more, though they thrust in return, making her flesh pebble deliciously with desire.

Mmmm… Yes…

All she wanted was to stay out there, away from land and the pressures of society, learning to love a monster she had not met in their true form yet. That would all come in time, however, and Atamai ran her fingers out along the "fronds" of tentacles swaying around her, stretching as if from the sea floor up towards the light of the surface. They waved and danced, playing with her, releasing somewhat their grip on her limbs so she could float and share her needs more freely.

Yet it was all about the moment, the experience, the otter deliberately letting air bubble from her mouth, watching the bubbles float away, almost mystically, back to the surface. She shook her head slowly, though it was little more than a light tip from one side to the other and back again, hunger rising in the pit of her belly.

Oh, how she needed them, out in the water, wherever the tentacles wanted to take her.

With an understanding in mind, the tentacles shifted again, pumping her pussy slowly, cautious of her body and its limits. She moaned, quivering – and gave herself to them once more.

With the ocean in her heart and the tentacles squeezing her form, holding her close, she could do nothing wrong in feeding desire.

Thank you for reading and I hope that everything was very much enjoyed!

Ready for more? Check out my author website for more furry fiction and where you can purchase my books!

https://linktr.ee/amethystmare

Cover art by Alena Bodrova.

Oisin Harrison blames his fiancée's distrust for ruining their relationship. He blames his father for pushing him into law school. But more than all that, he blames himself for letting other people's expectations stop him from going after his dream. But dressing in drag with his best friend is the one thing Oisin refuses to compromise.

As Sin, he meets handsome Trenton Fisher, a man who appreciates Oisin's cross-dressing. Trent upends his world by doing things to his body no one ever has, making him want more than just one night together. That is, until Oisin discovers his hot hookup works at his father's law firm and is angling for a promotion.

To complicate things, Trent doesn't seem to recognize Oisin out of drag. *Or does he?*

Will Oisin and Trent's magnetic attraction grow to something deeper, or will it threaten to jeopardize their careers and futures?

A NineStar Press Publication

Published by NineStar Press
P.O. Box 91792,
Albuquerque, New Mexico, 87199 USA.
www.ninestarpress.com

Waking Oisin

Printed in the USA
First Edition
February, 2018

Print ISBN: 978-1-948608-17-6

Also available in eBook, ISBN: 978-1-948608-09-1

Warning: This book contains sexually explicit content, which may only be suitable for mature readers.